Pie Comes
Before a Fall

Baker's Rise Mysteries Book Two

R. A. Hutchins

For my Nana A.
Who loved a good mystery story!
xxx

CONTENTS

If you follow this list in order, you will have made a perfect
Apple and Blackberry Pie *to enjoy while you read!*

ONE

Flora sank down into the armchair in her small sitting room with Reggie perched on her shoulder. A cup of chamomile tea sat on the table beside her, as she surveyed the room with pleasure. Tanya Hughes had just left, after helping Flora to sort the final boxes of clothes remaining from her move from London several months ago. It had taken them three weeks and quite a few evenings spent chatting and deciding which would go to charity and which would be sold at the stall which Tanya had suggested Flora have at the upcoming village fete.

As the new owner of the Baker's Rise estate, it fell to Flora to judge the many baking contests, so she would be too busy on the day to manage the stall, but Tanya had kindly agreed to do this for her. She was so relieved that her husband, Pat, had not lost his job as village policeman during the investigation into the murder of Harold Baker, when his rather laidback policing style had come under the scrutiny of his superiors. Instead, it had been the kick up the behind that he needed, and he had resumed his patrol of the village with renewed vigour in recent weeks, his trusty dog, Frank, by his side. So, on the day of the fete, Pat would be working to ensure no local youths stole a hot dog or tried to drink underage in Ray Dodds' beer tent. This left Tanya free to work on the clothes stall, and Flora had happily offered to give her a share of the profits on the day.

It was so lovely to see the room free of its clutter, that Flora sank into her armchair, for once totally relaxed. She pushed from her mind the first chapter of her novel, only half written on the vintage typewriter in the kitchen, the fact that Phil Stanton had been avoiding her since she all but accused him of Harold's murder, and the looming judging at the fete, which would no doubt ruffle some feathers and do nothing to raise her popularity amongst some of the women in the village. So, too, did she deliberately block out the uncomfortable memory of Enid Wright coming at her with an iron poker at the big house, before they were both covered in rubble from the collapsing ceiling, and the stir it had caused in the village when their vicar, the Reverend Wright, was also arrested along with his wife. He had defrauded the villagers out of money they thought was intended to fix the village roof, which had now been surveyed and found to be structurally without fault. Flora was confident that the next couple at the vicarage would be decidedly more suited to the role!

Instead, Flora stretched out her feet on the low leather footstool which she had cleaned up and brought down from the manor house, and leant her cheek into the soft downy feathers on Reggie's chest, enjoying the sound of his contented chirps and the feel of them rumbling through his little body. He had become even more her constant companion since saving her life that fateful day.

The scent of Tanya's musky perfume still floated in the air, making Flora think of Adam Bramble, and the pleasant evening they had shared together the previous weekend. A small smile formed on her lips as she remembered the dinner in Morpeth, how uncomfortable the detective had seemed in the fancy restaurant he had chosen for them, clearly trying to impress and please her, and how they had skipped dessert and gone for an ice cream by the river instead. They had walked through the park, arm in arm, and

Flora had felt a glow that had been missing for a long time. She didn't need fancy restaurants or posh evenings out – she had had enough of those in London to fill several lifetimes. No, all she wanted was some companionship and to feel a little less lonely. When they had parted at their parked cars, Bramble had pecked her sweetly on the lips, holding her hand and giving it a small squeeze before seeing Flora safely into her own vehicle. Flora sighed contentedly at the memory.

Finishing her tea, Flora extended her arm for Reggie to hop down to her hand. This had become their new nightly ritual, and she was trying to teach him some new phrases to replace the rather embarrassing vocabulary he had acquired from his late owner.

"Good boy, Reggie!" he squawked, anticipating her first words. Flora smiled in pleasure and repeated them back to him. She sometimes wondered who was teaching whom, not just with the speech but with the idea of being loved so unconditionally – even if it was by a feathered friend.

"Nice to see you!" Flora said, and waited to see if Reggie would copy her. She knew he could say the words, his ability to pick up different phrases was startlingly quick – uncanny even – but he often refused to do so on command. Flora could tell he was listening though, as his head was cocked to one side and his body completely still.

"She's a corker!" Reggie said eventually, rubbing his head against Flora's wrist. She couldn't help but grin.

"Thank you, Reggie, but let's try to be a bit more polite! How about, 'You're pretty!'"

"She's a cracker!" Reggie said, cheekily. Flora knew he was doing it on purpose, as was their nightly routine, so she simply moved on, tapping him once gently on the beak to convey displeasure.

"Welcome to the tearoom," Flora said slowly, "Welcome to the tearoom."

Reggie looked her straight in the eye, and Flora thought he might actually be memorising the phrase.

"Welcome... you old trout!" Flora had to stifle a giggle. Whilst the vocabulary Reggie had learned from Harold was sometimes amusing, it was certainly too rude for polite company, and she needed to be sure he wouldn't assail her customers with his eclectic repertoire.

"Reggie!" she scolded, "say 'tea-room, tea-room'" Flora split the word to make it easier for him to hear.

Reggie flew from her hand back to her shoulder and squawked quietly into Flora's ear, "she's a stunner," making her smile and forgive him his cheekiness, as she did every day.

TWO

The warm sun of late August shone down on Flora the next day, as she made her way along the small path which led from her home in the restored coach house down to the tearoom. Northeast England was having a small heatwave, and Flora was glad of it. The warmer temperatures in London were probably one of the few things she missed about the place. Reggie perched on her shoulder and bobbed up and down happily, his keen eyes looking into the trees and bushes on either side of the path. Flora had a spring in her step, as she had had what she believed to be the best idea of the summer so far! Keen to see her plan in motion, she had telephoned Betty Lafferty yesterday evening and asked her to meet at the Tearoom on The Rise first thing this morning. Collecting the day's baked goods from the side of the building which had previously been the stables, ensconced in the new plastic box which Flora had put there for this very purpose, she turned and waved as the new village post lady drove up the gravel driveway to deliver her mail.

The previous postie, Joe Stanton, had been relieved of his position once his bosses at Royal Mail heard of his tampering with the village post. According to Bramble, he was lucky that no criminal charges had been pressed against him for this, as well as for delivering Harold's blackmail letters. Unfortunately, the man still lived in the village, and Flora was far from being his favourite person – in fact, she avoided him like the plague. The new owner of the position, a friendly woman named Janet, always had a smile and a friendly word, and Flora had hit it off with her immediately.

After a quick chat, Flora let herself and Reggie into the tearoom, where he flew to his perch in the corner and she emptied the box of its baked goodies. Flora had just sat down with a pot of tea for two, anticipating Betty's arrival, when the woman herself appeared, her grey hair shining in the sunlight as she opened the door.

"Betty, thank you for coming up here so early!"

"It's nothing lass, Tina needs her morning walk, anyway."

Seeing the tiny terrier on a lead, being practically dragged into the room behind Betty, Reggie began to squawk loudly, "Tina the Terror! Tina the Terror!"

"Oh, do be quiet!" Flora chided him, but Reggie simply fluffed up his feathers and stared at her whilst repeating the same refrain until the little dog was safely hidden under the table.

Flora poured the tea and went to pop two teacakes into the toaster, knowing that Betty wouldn't refuse if offered.

"So lass, what can I help you with? You were a bit cryptic on the phone last night!"

"Well, Betty, the thing is, you were the chairwoman of the local Women's Institute for fifteen years, and you're a great baker."

"That's true," Betty preened as if she had her own feathers to fluff.

"And I'm a novice when it comes to baking. You see, I'm all too aware that the judging of the Scone Competition at the fete last year led to murder, quite literally... oh, I didn't mean you shouldn't have won!" Flora added hastily when she saw the older woman bristle, "It's just that I need there to be no questions over the judging this year. I know that it is my role as the new 'lady of the manor' so to speak, but it's not a cap I wear comfortably," Flora paused and took a breath, "What I'm trying to say is, will you do the judging with me for all of the cake categories? I'm going to ask Billy Northcote to help judge the Best in Bloom competition and Will Monkhouse to help with the Jolliest Pet. As the local vet, he has much more knowledge that me! Perhaps George Jones' wife, Pepper, can judge the pies with me, and maybe Lily Houghton will be up to help with the jams and chutneys?"

"What a great idea!" Betty blushed pink under her tight curls and Flora knew that her request had been met with approval. It had been a superb idea, even if she did think it herself, and also eliminated the awkwardness of having to judge Betty's creations, being as they were now good friends.

"That's settled then, it just means you won't be able to compete yourself…" Flora knew this might be the only sticking point, and tried to sneak it in at the end.

"Well, my dear, if it means helping you out, I'm willing to forgo the chance to show my skills," Betty said, making it clear she was doing Flora a favour. In reality, Flora could see how the woman's eyes sparkled at the thought of being a judge at the annual event, which held such high esteem in the village. "So," she said, her kind eyes staring straight into Flora's, "how are things with you and that handsome detective?"

It was Flora's turn to blush now, as she recounted their lovely date from the weekend and their plans to meet up as soon as possible after Flora had got her fete duties out of the way.

"Excellent, you deserve a bit of happiness," Betty patted Flora's hand before tucking into her toasted teacake, lathered in butter and jam. Flora could see her sneaking any pieces that didn't contain raisins to Tina under the table, but didn't have the heart to ask her to stop. Pets, as she herself was discovering, quite quickly became family.

Flora planned to pop to Billy Northcote's cottage in the village after shutting up the tearoom for the day. The only problem was that he lived on Cook's Row, just a few doors down from Phil, and Flora wanted to avoid bumping into that man at all costs. They had seen each other once since the awful confrontation in the tearoom, which Flora would much rather forget. It had certainly not been her finest moment, all but accusing the man of murder. So, when they had bumped into each other last week whilst both shopping in Baker's Rise Essential Supplies, Flora had turned on her heel in the middle of the tiny aisle and scurried in the other direction. Phil had thankfully blanked her completely, and they had both made a point of avoiding going to the small counter at the same time. Flora knew she should apologise to him for the insinuations she had made during the murder investigation, but hadn't been able to bring herself to seek Phil out after that one icy encounter.

So, now she sat at a table in the tearoom, the late-afternoon sun streaming through the windows, as Flora procrastinated over visiting Billy. She had gone over her lists of competitions for which she and Betty would be judges: Best Scone, Spongiest Sponge, Tastiest Treat, Most Victorious Victoria Sponge, Most Successful Free Style and Most Striking Showstopper Cake. Flora's heart beat faster in her chest just thinking about it. She knew she would come face to face with Edwina Edwards, the doctor's wife, at some point during the judging at the fayre. They had not got along since their first meeting, but the fact that Flora had had a hand in putting Edwina's cousin, Enid, behind bars for the murder of Harold must surely have added even more fuel to the woman's fiery dislike of her. Up until now, they had managed to avoid each other for the past month, but Flora knew that, as current chairwoman of the WI, Edwina wouldn't be able to resist entering her baked goods into the competition. It was a matter of personal honour for the woman, likewise for many amateur bakers in the area.

As the fete organisation committee had been headed up by the disgraced vicar and his wife, Flora had been asked to take over that role a few weeks ago. She only hoped that everything would run smoothly on the day, from the competitions to the live music, the children's games and the many stalls that would be present. As well as the stand selling her own clothes, Flora knew that Lily would be selling goods from the farm shop, whilst her husband was bringing some of his prize piglets to show the children. There would be the stall selling copies of the school photographs from years gone by, which Phil was presumably still organising, though Flora wasn't sure any more. Then there was to be a sweet stall, 'Baker's Rise Candy Surprise,' run by a young woman who was new to the village and had emailed Flora to ask if she could participate. Apparently, she was thinking of opening a shop by the same name on Front Street if there was enough interest. A group of Betty's friends, headed up by Jean whom owned Baker's Rise Essential Supplies, were setting up a crochet and knit sale, and of course there would be Ray Dodds and his massive beer tent.

Flora had enquired whether such a large marquee was required, for a village of their size, but Ray had given her question rather short shrift and informed Flora in no uncertain terms that it was normally the highlight of the event. Flora wasn't so sure, but she accepted what he said, provided the man himself took responsibility for the whole setting up and dismantling of the monstrosity, and for anyone who imbibed rather too much on the day. It was lucky that the event was always held on one of Stan Houghton's fallow fields, so there was plenty of room for everyone.

Flora stood and stretched, deciding now was as good a time as any to venture through the village to Cook's Row. She had the sudden idea – though it did seem mad – to take Reggie with her. It would bolster Flora's confidence to have him there, and she knew he travelled well on her shoulder. Decision made, Flora grabbed her handbag from its shelf behind the counter and made her way out into the sunshine.

THREE

As she had predicted, Reggie travelled beautifully on Flora's shoulder through the village, even sitting quietly when she met Harry Bentley and had a quick chat about the rents for the villagers. Flora had insisted that these be lowered in line with market rates, and the new payments were to come in force on the first of September. Satisfied that the partly-retired solicitor had it all in hand, Flora made her way quickly to Cook's Row.

The street sign had clearly been replaced in the past month – probably as a result of Pat Hughes' new project to clean up the village – but unfortunately the local youths had already had a go at the sign, adding an 'r' so that it now read 'Crook's Row.' Flora couldn't help but smile as she rushed past Phil's cottage and on to number eighteen, which Betty had confirmed was

Billy's address. As expected, the small front garden was a riot of roses and other flowers, all beautifully tended, and Flora's smile grew at the sight. She knocked lightly on the door, and waited with Reggie nuzzling into her neck.

"Ah, Mrs. Miller," Billy pulled open the door, a look of surprise and pleasure on his face, "What a lovely surprise!"

"Call me Flora, please, I was wondering if I might ask you a favour, Billy?"

"Of course, please do come in, but don't mind the mess!" By 'mess' Billy referred to a newspaper and tea cup on the side table. The rest of the room was spotless, small but cosy, with pictures of Billy, his wife and children on the mantel above the open fireplace. "I was hoping to see you, actually, to say thanks for that envelope young Harry Bentley brought round the other day. You didn't have to pay me for the bit of gardening, lass!"

"I did, and I was happy to," Flora squeezed his arm gently, eliciting a warm smile from the man, "it might not cover your salary for the past twenty years that you've worked for free, but I wanted you to have a good portion of it!"

Instead of sitting immediately, Flora went over to admire the photographs, several of which were the original black and white versions.

"Is this your wife?" Flora asked tentatively.

"Aye lass, that's my Mabel. Died six years ago this winter she did. Such a bonny woman. Love of my life she were."

"She is extremely pretty. How lucky you both were to have such a long marriage together," Flora said, somewhat wistfully, "and these are your children?"

"Aye, Christopher and Michael. Such good lads."

"Do they still live in the area?"

"No lass," Billy sighed heavily, the first time Flora had seen his mood anything less than upbeat since they met, "Chris is in America, and Michael down south in Cornwall."

"Do they ever visit?" Flora knew she might be pushing the conversation too far now.

"Not often, they have their own grown families now. Both grandfathers to their own grandkids."

"I'm sorry, Billy, that must be difficult."

"Aye well, I don't dwell, I've had a good life you know, and I couldn't expect them to stay in this tiny village – most of the young'uns leave eventually."

"Time for tea! Time for tea!" Reggie squawked from his chosen perch on the back of a wing backed chair. For once, Flora was grateful for the interruption.

"Aye, quite so," Billy chuckled, reaching over to stroke Reggie's downy head, "I'll get the kettle on!"

The smile on Billy's face, and the blush which had crept up from beneath his shirt collar when Flora had asked him to judge the flower competition at the fete, had made her whole day. Clearly her predecessor, Harold, had liked to keep the power all to himself, but Flora was enjoying sharing her responsibilities with her friends – it seemed like a win-win situation. Indeed, Flora was so deep in her happy thoughts as she headed back down Cook's Row an hour or so later, that she didn't see the tall man who turned the corner at the bottom of the street just before she herself reached it.

"Steady on," the barked command, and outstretched hand caught Flora off guard. That, and the shriek of "Stupid git!" which came from Reggie on her shoulder.

Flora stopped in her tracks, her heart beating wildly when she realised she was face to face with Phil. The temptation to simply step around him and avoid any confrontation was great, but Flora stood her ground, raising her eyes to his in a quiet challenge.

"Good afternoon, Flora," his tone was stilted, and Phil's eyes blazed.

"Hello, Phil," an awkward silence prevailed for several long seconds, as Flora gently tapped Reggie's beak to discourage another outburst.

"I hear you are judging at the fete?"

"I am. Are you still planning to run the old school photo stall?"

"I am. I've confirmed that the Morpeth Courier will come to take photographs."

"Excellent. Well, I had better be going."

"Ah, Flora," Phil hopped from one foot to the other uncomfortably.

"Yes?"

"I have been meaning to speak to you actually," Phil took in a deep breath.

"Really?"

"Yes… I, ah, I was hoping we could put all that unpleasantness behind us," his words spoke of reconciliation, but Phil's eyes still showed his residual anger.

"You were?" Flora couldn't hide the shock in her voice.

"Yes, I ah, I wanted to ask you a favour, actually," the reluctance in his tone spoke of how hard it had been for the man to make the request.

"A favour?" Flora was quite flabbergasted.

Phil seemed to lose his nerve. He stepped to the side to allow Flora to pass on the small pavement and kept his gaze fixed on his feet as he spoke, "Actually, can I call round another day? To the tearoom, I mean?"

"Well, yes, yes I suppose so," Flora's forehead bunched into a frown as she passed him, and Phil avoided meeting her eyes.

"Very good," he said as he continued in the other direction, leaving Flora both worried and intrigued as to what this favour could be. By the time she reached the coach house, having racked her brain for possibilities, Flora was still none the wiser, and decided to put it out of her head. He had shown himself to be quite a volatile character, so Flora hoped Phil might just forget his request altogether.

FOUR

Flora was exhausted. She had spent the whole day helping set up the fete and overseeing each stall and tent, leaving the tearoom in the capable hands of Tanya and Betty. It was half past four in the afternoon, and she was finally confident that everything was in place, with the exception of the candy stall, whose table stood empty and unadorned. As the fete was tomorrow, Flora wondered if the lady who had requested the spot had changed her mind. The tent where most of the judging would take place had been erected by Stan Houghton and a couple of his farm hands, before Flora and Amy had decorated it with fairy lights and bunting. It looked very pretty, even if she did say so herself!

A tap on her shoulder brought Flora back from her tired musings, and she turned to find an elegant young woman, with long, shiny brown hair tied up into a high ponytail. She looked like someone in their early twenties, but had the confidant air of someone older.

"Sorry to startle you. The large man over there," she pointed to Ray in the beer tent, "told me that you're the lady in charge. I'm Emma. Emma Blenkinsopp, I sent an email about the sweet stall…"

"Oh yes, Emma! Hello! I was just thinking about this empty stall here," Flora indicated the trestle table and fold-out display wall behind it, "it's all yours!"

"Oh! Thank you! I'm sorry I'm late, I.., well, I almost had second thoughts," a frown covered the younger woman's face, until her whole visage changed with it, making her appear much older and world-weary.

"Don't worry, I'm always getting cold feet about new ventures," Flora reassured her, "Please let me know if you need any help setting up." Secretly, though, Flora hoped she wouldn't be called upon that day. She had plans to disappear home for a glass of red wine and to reheat last night's lasagne.

"Ooh, she's a corker! She's a corker!" The piercing refrain could be heard getting closer as Reggie flew over from his perch beside the organiser's table, which Flora had set up to try to keep her on track on the actual day of the fete.

"Oh, who's this lovely chap?" Rather than being frightened by the energetic green bird who had appeared out of nowhere to land on Flora's shoulder, Emma seemed enchanted by Reggie, reaching out immediately to stroke him with a delicate, white-gloved hand – clearly prepared for handling food and not errant birds! Reggie fussed and preened, accepting her attention as if it were exactly the way he should be treated by everyone!

"Careful, you'll never get rid of him tomorrow if you give him an excuse!" Flora laughed, as Reggie happily jumped to Emma's outstretched hand, nuzzling her palm.

"Oh, I wouldn't mind a little helper, as long as he doesn't eat all the sweets and chocolates!" Emma giggled, clearly enchanted by the animal.

When Flora managed to drag Reggie away from his new friend, she wandered over to the beer tent where Ray and Shona had been hard at work all day. Despite her efforts, Shona remained fresh-faced, her long, brown hair pulled up into a messy bun on top of her head. Flora subconsciously touched her own neglected locks, which she had intended to get trimmed and dyed before the event, but somehow never gotten around to. She felt like the ever-increasing greys were beating her into submission. Though, to be fair, the worse it got, the less she cared about her appearance.

A long table had been set out with dozens of clean, upturned glasses, whilst Ray was putting the finishing touches to his menu on a large chalkboard.

"Oh, I didn't know you were serving food as well?" Flora asked, squinting to read the details of the pies that would be on offer.

"Aye, I've got a new supplier, and the pies are right tasty. I want to take advantage of the crowds tomorrow for the villagers to try the pub's new offering."

"A new supplier? So, not George Jones then? I thought you'd been serving his pies for years?"

"Aye well, a change is as good as a rest, as they say," Ray winked at her then, sending Flora scuttling over to the other side of the tent, where Reggie was perched on a chair watching Shona set out the last of the tables and benches for customers. Will Monkhouse, the local vet, was standing holding the other end of the wooden seat, helping Shona position the bench carefully. Once it was lowered to the ground, Will came over and put his arm around Shona's waist casually, as the pair smiled at Flora.

Flora herself hid any surprise at their obvious closeness – this was a relationship she hadn't heard about on the local grapevine, "Hello Will, thanks for helping out," she said, having already thanked Shona earlier in the day.

"It's no problem, I'm happy to help this lovely lady here," he said, pecking Shona on the cheek and being rewarded with a blush in return.

"I have to rush off," Shona said, checking her watch, "the childminder only has Aaron till five today!"

"Of course," Flora smiled as Will hurried to get Shona's coat and bag for her from the back of the tent.

"Thanks again for asking me to help judge the pet contests!" Will seemed such an amiable chap, Flora was always relaxed in his presence – provided he wasn't talking about his favourite bovine subject, of course. Cow ailments weren't exactly Flora's cup of tea!

"It is me who is grateful, really, thank you," Flora said, as Shona took Will's hand, shouted goodbye to her dad, and the sweet couple left the tent together.

Flora gave a small sigh of longing at the sight of the

pair, calling loudly for Reggie and heading off quickly, before Ray could strike up conversation again. She had planned to go up to the manor house, to see how the builders were fairing on fixing up the ceiling that had collapsed a month ago, but her tired feet were screaming, even in the floral wellington boots which Flora was wearing. For once, she had chosen practicality over style, and for the most part had been glad of it. Except now, having been on her feet all day, Flora was desperate to sit down. The manor house would have to wait till after the fete. Now that she had finally received her divorce money, Flora was keen to plough ahead with the structural fixes which she could afford, at the very least to make the place safe enough for her to begin the job of sorting the remnants of Harold's life again.

First things first, though, she had the highlight of the village calendar to not just get through, but to make a success! Flora desperately hoped it would be memorable for all the right reasons.

FIVE

Flora was happier than she'd like to admit that the day of the fete had dawned sunny and warm, and had stayed so throughout the whole day. Relaxing at home after the event, with a well-earned glass of vino and her tired feet in a bucket of warm, lavender-scented water, Flora rested her head back on the comfortable chair beside the fire and listened to Reggie's contented snores. He had received so much attention from children and adults alike at the fayre, not least because he had spent most of the day perched at Emma's candy stall, that even he was quite worn out now!

The judging had gone well, and, more importantly to Flora, had been deemed to be fair and proper. The music from a local folk band had been perfect for the occasion and there had been plenty of visitors from neighbouring villages to bump up the numbers in attendance. Tanya had reported excellent sales from the clothes stall and Phil had looked relaxed talking to the local press about the vintage school photos. Flora herself had tried to avoid the newspaper crew at all costs, but had at last been cornered after judging the roses with Billy. She had given a small, awkward interview, which Flora hoped would be cut out completely in the final edits!

All in all it had been a great day. Well, apart from that small cloud on the horizon of Flora's memory...

Fresh from judging the Most Victorious Victoria Sponge competition, and secretly revelling in the fact that Betty had judged Edwina Edward's effort only worthy of second place, Flora's attention had been caught by shouting in the beer tent. Expecting it to be some drunken youths, Flora had rushed over hoping to already find Pat Hughes at the scene. Instead, she saw an older woman shrieking at Ray, her peroxide blonde hair bobbing up and down in her evident anger. The woman was small in stature, but certainly made up for it in volume, with her accusations being heard from all around.

"You're a liar, Ray Dodds! A sweaty, slimy liar, and I don't know what I was even thinking to have married you all those years ago!"

"We've been divorced for over twenty-five years, woman!"

"Aye, and here your two sons are, asking you for a job in the pub or the kitchen, and you're refusing! You wouldn't have even known they were yours if I hadn't told you! You haven't seen the twins since they were four years old!" On and on she went, and the pair were attracting quite an audience.

Clearly not embarrassed, Ray shouted back, "Well, you're the one who left, taking them with you, just like all the others before and after you! Besides, what are they now? Thirty? They should already be settled by now, not scrounging jobs off me!"

"You should be ashamed man, what kind of father are you? No kind, that's what! And did you even know Patricia has died?"

"He is a good father," it was Shona who interrupted them now, her face unusually taut and white, as she carried a tray of dirty glasses.

"Well, one day you'll see the truth!" the woman spat back at her, before linking arms with the two tall men who flanked her one on either side, and sauntering out of the tent, as eloquently as she could manage with high heels that kept getting stuck in the mud.

Both Ray and Shona had watched the woman leave in silence, until Shona put down the tray on the nearest table and slowly turned back to face her father, "Every year! Every year, Dad," she shouted, causing Flora to raise her eyebrows in surprise, having never heard more than a quiet word from the usually amiable young woman, "Every year I have to face this embarrassment when another of your exes comes out of the woodwork! People you've never mentioned, siblings I never even knew existed!"

Shona had shouted and railed, clearly getting out a lot of the feelings she'd had bottled up for a long time. It took Will coming over from the sheep pens to calm her, before the young woman had eventually stopped.

"You should be ashamed!" the local vet had said to Ray, loud enough for all to hear, before he led Shona out of the tent.

Ray had carried on as normal, serving drinks and making jokey banter, but Flora had observed the sheen of sweat over his brow, heavier than normal, and the slight shake to the man's hands.

Pushing the memory from her mind, Flora decided to focus on happy things – like the fact the event was over for another year! There would be the annual talent show at Christmas, but apparently George's wife, Pepper Jones, normally organised that. Flora took a sip of her wine and let her eyes drift shut, until she was rudely brought back to the present by a loud hammering on her front door.

"What the..?" Flora muttered, reluctantly taking her wet feet out of the bowl and drying them off quickly with the towel she had over her lap for that purpose.

"Shut yer face! Shut yer face!" Reggie, startled from his sleep, shrieked in the direction of the hammering, which persisted as Flora hurried to the front door. For once, Reggie stayed where he was and didn't follow.

"This had better be important!" Flora muttered under her breath, unlocking the door and pulling it open to reveal none other than Phil Drayford. Flora didn't bother to try to mask her shock at the man's appearance on her doorstep, too annoyed was she by his intrusion into her private relaxation.

"Sorry, Flora, I ah…" he trailed off, shoving his hands in his pockets and staring down at Flora's bare feet. Apparently, what had been important enough to come here for, to hammer on the door for, was no longer quite so pressing.

"Is it about the fete, Phil? About the stall?" Flora tried to prompt the man, desperate as she was to get back to her comfortable chair. She made a point of not inviting him in.

"Ah, not exactly. Well, yes, but not in the way you think. May I come in?"

Flora sighed heavily and took in the man's bedraggled features. His hair stuck up where he had obviously run his hands through it one too many times, and his shirt was creased and stained with sweat. Flora decided, almost against her better judgement, to take pity on him and reluctantly invited Phil in, knowing fine well what Reggie would have to say about it!

SIX

"Here's the fool! Here's the fool!" Reggie couldn't contain his anger that not only had his snoozing been disturbed, but it was Phil – whom he had a particular dislike for – who was responsible!

"Reggie, shush, quiet or cage!" Flora warned in her most severe voice, though secretly she shared her feathered friend's sentiments.

"Sorry to intrude," Phil said, taking the offered seat on the sofa. Flora deliberated internally with whether or not to offer him a drink. Her own, half-drunk wine glass sat on the coffee table, and she decided disappointedly that it would be rude not to offer.

"Oh, no thanks, Flora, I'm not intending to stay," Phil ran his hands down his thighs distractedly as Flora resumed her earlier seat on her favourite armchair, feeling better in the knowledge that this was to be a quick visit.

"Then how can I help you? Did you get many sales on the photo stall?"

"The stall?" Phil seemed unsure what Flora was referring to for a moment, until his brain kicked back in, "Ah, yes, I'll have all the ordered copies made and sent out within the fortnight. Should hopefully raise the school's prospects with Northumberland council. The new term starts in a week, and there are still rumblings we'll be closed by Christmas."

"I'm sorry to hear that, but if the stall was successful and everything went smoothly then..?"

"Did you see that blonde woman with the two dodgy-looking blokes? The ones who were hanging round the beer tent for ages before she had the showdown with Ray?"

"I, ah," Flora struggled to keep up with the change in topic, tired as she was, "yes, well, I heard her before I saw her!"

"Well, it's not the woman actually, it's... did you get a good look at them? The men, I mean?"

"No, sorry," Flora had no idea where this was going,

"um, pardon me, but is this related to your request for a favour the other day or is it something else entirely?" Flora dearly wished he would get the point.

"Yes, actually, well a couple of people remarked that they'd thought it was me with the woman, until they'd looked closely. They said I look just like those men, right down to facial features, you see. So, I went to see for myself, and lo and behold the likeness was clear even to me!"

"I'm sorry, Phil, I didn't… I mean I don't see how…"

"Do you remember the time you confronted me in the tearoom. About Harold's murder?"

How could she forget? But Flora didn't know why he would mention it now, "Well, yes, and I am sorry, Phil, I…"

"Yes, no matter, it's not an apology I want," he was getting more erratic now, shoving his fingers through his hair, "do you remember what I blurted out then? About Harold's holding it over me that my dad might not be… my real father."

"I remember," Flora whispered, having a sinking feeling now that she might have guessed where this was going.

"Well, if those were Ray's estranged sons, and I look like them, it doesn't take much to put the two together and…"

"And?" Flora was frozen, her hands clasped in her lap. Even Reggie was eerily silent.

"And I need to see the file that Harold had on me. The one from up at the big house. And the files on my dad and Ray for that matter. Have the police finished with the documents yet?"

Flora let out a long sigh, to buy time more than anything else, "The police have returned all the paperwork that is not being kept as evidence, yes, but I've decided not to look through those files, Phil. I have stored them at a secure location, away from here, away from the manor house too, where I know they'll be safe. I didn't read them, and I don't intend to. I'm not like Harold."

"I know that Flora, I know," his face softened, and Phil looked at her beseechingly, "I just have to find out. It must be in there. The truth."

"Remember, Phil," Flora said gently, "those files just contain Harold's truth. He was a bitter old man. There may be nothing to substantiate his claims."

R. A. Hutchins

"Yes, but he was right about the vicar…"

"That's as may be, but maybe some of the stuff was just conjecture?"

"Still, I need to see who he thought my father was."

"I'm sorry, Phil, I can't get that file for you, or anyone else," Flora tried to hide the nerves she felt fluttering in her stomach, not knowing how Phil would react to her refusal. She clearly recalled having a quick look at Alf Drayford's file when she had first found the secret room at the manor house, and seeing the photos of the man kissing a woman who was presumably not his wife. Whether this was his first extra-marital dalliance or not, Flora didn't know, but it was certainly possible that if Phil's mother had found out about her husband's cheating early in their marriage, then perhaps she would have had her own affair in retaliation. None of this Flora intended to share with Phil, however – those files were a curse, to be sure.

"Please, Flora, just this one thing, then I won't bother you again!" Phil stood and began pacing back and forth like a caged animal.

Flora rose from her seat, slowly, and began to back out of the room. Reggie flew to her shoulder protectively, "I won't change my mind," she said firmly, hurrying then to the front door and opening it.

In a moment, Phil stormed past, without so much as looking at Flora, and out into the cool night air. His face was red with anger, his eyes bulbous, and Flora was relieved to quickly shut the door behind him. Sinking her back against the cool wood, Flora let out a sigh of relief, as Reggie squawked "Now there's trouble!" echoing her sentiments exactly.

SEVEN

Flora ambled around the duck pond, taking time to admire the two beautiful swans which were new arrivals to the Green. She hoped they would linger, as their graceful presence made a perfect addition to the idyllic scene. It was Sunday, the day after the fete and Phil's memorable exit from her home. Flora couldn't help but sigh at the thought, hoping she wouldn't see him in church.

The day was warm already, and held great promise for a hot afternoon, so Flora wore one of her favourite sundresses, dotted with tiny, embroidered daisies – it would be perfect for meeting Adam in the pub later that afternoon, as they'd arranged. Before that though, church beckoned, followed by a lovely Sunday lunch with Betty and Harry. Flora smiled as she saw their new interim vicar waiting to greet her in the church porch. Unlike his predecessor, Reverend Marshall was a younger, seemingly happy man, and Flora had not seen him without a smile on his face these past two weeks since he and his lovely family had arrived. Newly returned from missionary work in Africa, they had been looking for lodging and a new post, and the vacancy in Baker's Rise had come up quite unexpectedly, what with the previous vicar and his wife being arrested! Flora had welcomed James, his wife Sally, and their three young daughters to the tearoom the previous weekend, and had been glad to also see them at the fete yesterday. Perhaps they were the breath of fresh air which the village so badly needed? Flora hoped so.

"Mrs. Miller, beautiful day!"

"Indeed it is, Vicar..."

"Daddy, Daddy, Megan has been running up the aisle again!" they were interrupted by Reverend Marshall's eldest daughter, Evie, who had a penchant for telling tales.

"Yes, dear, Daddy's working right now," the reverend muttered, though still not losing his smile. Flora had already deduced that he doted on the four women in his life.

"But Daddy, the ladies are tut-tut-tutting!"

"Perhaps, you can come and show me," Flora interjected, hoping to offer some aid to the situation.

"Thank you so much, Mrs. Miller, my wife has unfortunately been struck down with a migraine today," Reverent Marshall raised his eyebrows and gave a rueful smile, before ruffling his daughter's red curls and turning to greet the next parishioner.

True to Evie's word, little Megan, who must be all of four years old, was charging down the aisle pretending to be a space rocket. Flora tried to hide her smile behind her hand, as Evie pointed to the disgraceful deed. Their middle sister, Charlotte, sat on the front pew with her nose in a picture book, oblivious to the scene. The small group of assembled churchgoers were not so oblivious, however, with Edwina Edwards being quite vocal about her disapproval.

"Evie, would you like me to tell you a story about travelling in space?" Flora whispered, as the girl was about to charge past her for the second time.

"Ooh, a story?"

"Yes, it's about a parrot who goes into space!" It was the first thing that came into Flora's head.

"I would like that! Did you bring the cakes from your shop?"

"The tearoom? Oh no, honey, I don't carry them about with me!" Flora grinned broadly now, and sat on the second pew, with the little girl hopping up onto her lap without invitation. Evie sat down with Charlotte in front of them, as Betty and Harry came to sit alongside Flora. As she improvised a story, Flora felt a sense of contentment which she had not felt in a long while.

The service finished, and pleasantries exchanged with their neighbours, Flora, Betty and Harry walked the short distance to Betty's cottage for lunch.

"It's so hot, I thought we'd just have salad today," Betty said, casting a sideways glance to Harry who walked behind the two women on the narrow street.

"Oh, I well, I…"Harry stuttered.

Betty gave a tinkling laugh and stopped to face him, "Catch you out every time, I do, Harry Bentley. It's Sunday! Of course, it's a roast with all the trimmings!"

Flora ran her hand surreptitiously over her stomach, thinking perhaps salad might not have been such a bad idea. She had tried two different types of Ray's new

pies at the fete the day before and both had been
delicious, but the Steak and Ale had been her favourite.
She had had to hide her plate under the organisation
table, though, to avoid the glares coming from George
and Pepper over on their Baker's Rise Pastries and Pies
stall. It had all been rather awkward. The pies
though... well, they would surely be adding inches to
her waistline in the winter months to come – comfort
food to be sure!

Harry patted his stomach and leaned back in his chair,
wiping his mouth with a napkin, "Well my dear, you
have outdone yourself this week, Betty my love!" Betty
leaned imperceptibly towards the man and blushed at
his words. To cover her embarrassment, she stood and
began clearing the plates, tossing a small piece of
leftover chicken to Tina, who waited hopefully under
the table.

"No, I'll do that," Harry winked at them, "give you
two ladies a chance to chat!"

Flora smiled up at him, before turning to Betty, "So,
did you enjoy the fete?"

"Aye, lass, had a great time judging those cakes, I did!
I'm up for next year if you need me?"

"Of course, consider yourself booked annually!"

"Really? Thank you! But, tell me, did you hear that ruckus from the beer tent? So unseemly, airing your dirty laundry in public like that!"

"I did, I saw it actually. The woman was boiling with rage."

"Aye, Gloria always did have a temper on her. She was wife number three, before Shona's mum, Wendy, then there was Patricia. I think there was some crossover between them, if you know what I mean!"

"Oh, yes, I can imagine," though Flora didn't really want to imagine any of Ray's amorous liaisons, "and they all left the village?"

"Yes, I don't think any of them could bear having his latest attraction paraded in front of them. It's a small village, you know?"

"Oh yes, I know," Flora thought of Phil but said nothing further.

"They all took their kids with them too, and only Shona kept in contact with her dad. Then she moved back here when she was... well, she must've been about nineteen and pregnant with Aaron she was. To give him his dues, Ray took her straight in without a word of disapproval. Well, he couldn't really say anything, could he, not with his history!" Betty chuckled and stood up as Harry came into the room.

"I'll have to love you and leave you, ladies, I'm afraid, as there's a bowls game at four o'clock and Billy Northcote will skin me alive if I'm late! That Witherham lot beat us last month, so we need to win it back today!"

"You boys and your games," Betty said, her face a picture of besotted indulgence.

"Oh, before I forget Flora," Harry turned as he reached the front door, "a young woman approached me at the fayre yesterday, enquiring about leasing the empty shop that the Estate owns on Front Street. Sweets, I think she wanted to sell – had that pretty stall at the fete. Anyway, I said we'd look into it on Monday, you and I. Bye for now," he leant in and pecked Betty on the cheek, earning him a small, embarrassed shove on the arm. Flora smiled at the pair, making her all the more restless to see Adam in an hour.

EIGHT

The Bun in the Oven was quite packed that Sunday afternoon, with the village still apparently buzzing from the previous day's fete. Flora and Adam were lucky to find a free table, though it did mean they were perched next to the back entrance, where anyone needing to use the bathroom facilities had to walk past them. It mattered not a jot to Flora, though, who felt as if she was floating in Adam's company. Walking through the door to the pub, her arm linked in his, she had felt special and appreciated. Even more so when he pulled her chair out in a gentlemanly fashion, and asked her drink preference before going to the bar to order for them both.

Flora took a moment to cast her eyes around the dim interior. George and Pepper Jones sat at the next table, and had said a quick hello when Flora and Adam entered, but seemed to be engaged in some sort of marital dispute – the tension was coming off the pair in waves, and they were studiously avoiding looking at each other. Feeling rather uncomfortable, and as if she were intruding, Flora quickly turned her attention back to the bar, where she spotted Doctor Edwards waiting to order for him and Edwina. There was no sign of the woman herself, however, nor of their host, for that matter. Ray seemed to be distinctly absent, and the queue for drinks and Sunday food was growing.

Flora decided to take the moment to use the bathroom, so left her coat on her chair to reserve the table and slipped out of the door beside her. The narrow corridor was painted in a dull grey hue which was peeling badly, and had perhaps once been blue. A shiver ran up Flora's spine, partly from the chill, and partly from the sparsity of the place, which had the musty smell of rising damp. The toilets were located near the back door to the building, and one had to first pass the entrance to the behind-the-bar area, from where there were steps down to the beer cellar. Unable to help herself, Flora paused when she heard raised voices coming from that direction. The door to her left was ajar, and Flora peered around it, shocked when she saw Edwina Edwards standing facing Ray.

"I've told you, I've got to get the pies! For goodness

sake, woman!"

"Oh come on, Ray, you've been after me for years, we both know it!"

"I told you when you come here that morning Harold died, I'm not interested. Your husband's my cousin!"

"Second cousin once removed or some such nonsense!" her voice rose as she pressed herself against him.

"Enough woman!" Ray moved out of view, and a somewhat shocked Flora made a hasty trip to the bathroom, really wishing she hadn't just witnessed that embarrassing exchange. On her way back to the main area of the pub all was quiet, and Flora found that Adam had just been served by Shona, who must've appeared from the flat upstairs. She didn't normally work Sundays, preferring to spend the time with her young son, Aaron.

"Thank you," Flora whispered, noting that Edwina still had not reappeared – the doctor sat alone, somewhat morosely, at a table by the window.

"I might, ah, just take advantage of the facilities, myself," Adam said, before Flora could tell him what she had seen and overheard.

The bar was quiet again, and Shona had disappeared,

presumably back upstairs, so Flora fingered the stem of her wine glass, thinking of Reggie and hoping he wasn't too lonely at home all this time. Tanya came in at that moment with Pat and, seeing Flora, made a beeline straight for her whilst her husband went to wait at the bar.

"Don't worry, Flora, I know you have a big date! I just wanted to say that I have the money from the clothes stall, all counted up!" Tanya smiled widely.

"Oh, you're a star, thank you. Do you want to drop by with it to the tearoom tomorrow morning? I can give you your share and we can have a proper catch-up?"

"I'll look forward to it," Tanya winked, a large obvious gesture, in the direction of Adam who was returning from the bathroom. He had been gone a while, though the fact only just now dawned on Flora.

"You'll never guess what I saw!" they laughed, as both had said exactly the same thing at the same moment.

"You go first," Flora encouraged.

"Well, I was on my way back from the loo, when I heard raised voices…"

"It wasn't Edwina again was it?"

"Edwina? No, it was Ray shouting at Shona. I could only see the top of his head and the back of hers from the angle they stood at the top of the cellar stairs, but he was saying, 'Do you know how many kids I have, you're just one of many!' Poor girl, I wonder why she stays with him."

"That is sad. They normally seem to get on so well. Apart from the showdown at the fete yesterday…"

"Showdown?"

Flora filled Adam in on the events at the fayre, with Ray's ex-wife and sons, and Shona's anger at her father, before going on to tell him what she'd overheard between Edwina and Ray.

"No!" Adam chuckled under his breath, "Well I never! And she comes across as so prim and proper!"

They both laughed then and lifted their glasses to take a sip, when an almighty scream filled the room.

"Dad! No! Dad!" Shona's high pitched sobs and screams rent the air, and in a heartbeat Adam and Pat Hughes were both through the back door and into the area behind the bar. Unable to help herself, as if her legs had a mind of their own, Flora followed them. She had never been back here before – in fact the first time she had even seen into the area was just now when she spied Edwina with Ray. One staircase led up to what must be the apartment above the pub, and the other, closer staircase, led down into the cellar. These stairs going down were not carpeted, and were simply hard concrete.

Shona stood, halfway up them, her face white as a sheet, her whole body trembling. Adam helped her up the remaining steps, where Flora gave her a hug, as the two men descended into the cellar.

"I only went to check on why he was taking so long," Shona whispered, her lip quivering and tears streaming down her face, "I was mad that I'd had to leave Aaron and come downstairs to help out."

"Shush now, don't say anything more," Flora said, leading Shona further away, and hoping that the younger woman hadn't just implicated herself in anything. She had a sense that things were going to get very bad from here on in.

NINE

Flora could hear Adam on his phone, requesting backup, as Tanya came from the bar and led Shona away to get her a strong drink. Again, Flora's curiosity got the better of her, and she found herself going down the stairs. When she reached the bottom, however, what she saw made her wish that she hadn't. Ray lay there, on his back, in a pool of blood that encircled his head like a ghastly halo, a pile of frozen pies surrounding him. His skull was dented on one side, matching a pie dish which lay next to him, that was half squashed.

"Is he definitely...?"

"He's dead, love, go on back up," Adam admonished her gently, "Cracked his skull on the concrete when he fell backwards by the look of it, but I imagine it was a blow from that pie that sent him flying in the first place."

Flora turned to do as she was instructed, as Dr.
Edwards made his way tentatively down the stairs.
Sirens could be heard from outside, in sharp contrast to
the deathly silence in the bar area as she entered it.

Other than Shona's sobbing, only one voice broke the
shocked quiet of the room – George Jones, who could
clearly be heard muttering, "That's what you get for
buying inferior pies!"

Flora sent a shocked glare his way, biting her tongue
on the retort, 'What? Murdered?' which she dearly
wished to bark at him.

"Tell them that no one is to leave!" Bramble shouted
back up, and Flora relayed his instructions to all those
assembled. Sitting down at her table, where Tanya was
consoling Shona, Flora took several gulps of her wine,
before deciding it was far too reminiscent of the blood
she had just seen. Her stomach heaved and Betty's
Sunday lunch threatened to make a reappearance, so
Flora rushed back along to the toilet, grateful for the
fresh air from the back door to the building, which was
now open and swaying back and forth.

Several long and difficult hours later, Flora opened the door to the coach house to let herself, Tanya and Aaron in. Shona had been taken to the police headquarters in Morpeth to be interviewed, with Bramble and Detective Blackett, who had appeared on the scene like a dark raven heralding bad news. Pat Hughes had also accompanied them, to give Shona some moral support, as he saw it as his duty as local policeman. So, Flora and Tanya had reassured a hysterical Shona that they would look after Aaron until she returned and they were allowed back into the pub again. Flora had a small second bedroom, a box room really, which was currently filled with the shoes and coats she had insisted on keeping. It had a pull-out sofa bed, though, that was easily big enough for a young boy, should it come to him having to stay the night.

Flora really had very little experience with children, and was glad of Tanya's help in reassuring Aaron. He had been ushered downstairs and out of the pub so fast, that he had seen nothing of importance. However, the police cars and forensics team, as well as the uniformed officers making their enquiries with everyone inside the building, were enough to set his warning bells ringing. As a result, the lad had cried silently the whole walk here, despite Flora's promises that he could have a turn on her special typewriter and even play with Reggie if he liked.

Seeming to sense their mood, Reggie flew straight to Flora's shoulder and nuzzled her neck, "Missed you," he squawked, accepting Aaron's strokes to his head eagerly.

"Missed you, too," Flora whispered back, trying to lock the wooden front door behind them and realising that her fingers were still shaking from the afternoon's events.

When Aaron was settled at the typewriter at the kitchen table, with a slice of apple pie from Flora's selection of cakes – leftovers from the tearoom which needed eating - and a glass of milk, with instructions to shout if he needed any help, Flora and Tanya finally took the weight off their feet in the sitting room.

"Well, that was a day," Tanya said quietly, decidedly more subdued than normal. In fact, Flora noted, the woman had barely spoken at all since the police descended on the scene.

"It certainly was," Flora replied gently, "I never want to see something like that again!"

"It must've been awful," Tanya replied, but Flora could see that her mind was still elsewhere. She wondered if she could broach the subject, delicately.

"The sight of so many police officers always scares me a little," Flora began, "even when I know I have done nothing wrong. It was the same when they came to the village to investigate poor Harold's death."

"Tell me about it," Tanya whispered, her eyes filling with tears.

"Oh Tanya," Flora stood up from her armchair and joined her friend on the sofa, putting her arm around Tanya's thin shoulders, over the cerise pink and leopard skin mohair sweater she wore.

"I'm okay, thank you Flora, it is just my past catching up with me. My ex – the one in London, the Russian I told you a bit about – well, he was into some bad stuff. Criminal things. I always lived in fear the police would come knocking. I told him I wanted to know nothing of his dealings, but I always worried that if it came to it the police wouldn't believe that I wasn't a part of it all. When I left – it was in such a hurry, I ran away, you see – I took the first train North, and ended up in Newcastle-upon-Tyne. I had nowhere to go, and very little money, so I sat in a café at the train station with a cold cup of tea for two hours, until I caught a man at the counter looking at me. Of course, I thought he must be a policeman, searching for me, or some undercover

investigator hired quickly by Dmitriy. I was so
paranoid, but in the end I was half right – it was Pat.
We got talking, and that is history. He offered me the
protection and the quiet life I was desperate for,
somewhere I wasn't likely to be found, and I offered
him companionship."

"Well," Flora wasn't sure what to say. She was very
keen to know if the couple loved each other, but knew
it was none of her business, "how long have you been
together?"

"Four years this December. I just couldn't bear to see in
a new year in the same situation, so I ran in the middle
of winter."

They were interrupted then by Aaron, who joined
them in the sitting room, Reggie on his shoulder. The
bird had become quickly attached to the lad, and Flora
was glad of it. Anything to make the boy feel more
settled and secure. It was dark outside, and Tanya had
finished her fruit tea.

"I had better be getting home, if you two will be
okay?" Tanya stood and stretched, trying to dry her
eyes surreptitiously.

"Of course, thank you so much for your help," Flora
stood and gave Tanya a big hug, before seeing her to

the door. Aaron would stay the night, and they would see where things stood in the morning. Flora hoped Adam would text her, but she didn't want to send him a message in case he was still embroiled in the investigation. Even though he had been off duty, he was still the D.I. best placed to investigate as he had been first on the scene and was coming to know the village and its inhabitants well.

"Well, Aaron," Flora said, as they waved Tanya off down the small path to the main driveway, "when I was at church earlier today, I told the Marshall girls a story about a certain green and yellow parrot who went into space!"

"Reggie?" The boy's eyes lit up for the first time since they'd arrived back.

"Yes, would you like to hear it?"

After repeating a version of Reggie's space adventure, plus one to Buckingham Palace, and one where he was a pirate's parrot, Aaron's eyelids were drooping, and Flora too was completely exhausted. A small seed had taken root in her mind, however, as she made up the tales on the spot, that these stories came to her much more easily than the romance novel she had been trying – rather unsuccessfully – to write. What if she wrote these instead, and found an illustrator and…?

Flora's chain of thought was interrupted by her phone buzzing with an incoming message. She laid a blanket over Aaron, as he slept against the arm of the sofa, thinking she would move him to his makeshift bed once she had made it up. The text message was from Adam, saying that he was staying at police headquarters in Morpeth overnight, where he and Blackett were interviewing Shona. He said that Shona herself was bearing up as well as could be expected, and that he would give her a lift back to the village in the morning, when she had finished helping them with their enquiries. He added two kisses to the end of his message – the only indication that it was anything but a formal, work-related text – which Flora fixated on for a good few minutes, before dragging her weary body off to the spare room to get it set up for Aaron.

Poor Shona, Flora thought to herself as she gathered up her clothes and accessories and took them through to lay over a small chair in her own bedroom. Despite it being only the end of August, there was a chill in the air, and Flora went to the kitchen to turn on the central heating. Reggie followed her from room to room, clearly as unsettled by the change to their routine as she herself was. Flora knew things didn't look good for Shona, what with Adam having seen her arguing with her father just before he was murdered, yet she just couldn't bring herself to believe that Shona had done it. *No, there has to be another explanation,* Flora decided resolutely, and promised herself there and then that she would discover the truth and clear Shona's name in the process.

TEN

The tearoom was buzzing with activity on Monday morning, with Tanya, Betty, and Lily Houghton from the farm all having arrived just after opening, to discuss the events of the previous day – news travels fast in a small community, bad news even faster. Aaron sat in the back corner, playing with Reggie and enjoying a toasted teacake, while the women whispered at the front of the shop, trying to appear inconspicuous to the boy.

"Well, two mur... two of these events in the village in as many months. It's unheard of!" Lily exclaimed, being careful to moderate her vocabulary when Flora gave a pointed look in the direction of Aaron. Despite them keeping their voices low, Flora was worried he would overhear.

"It's not two in two months, though, is it?" Betty

chimed in, "Because Harold was offed a good ten months before Flora here realised it had been foul play!"

"True, true," Lily conceded, "still it's a lot for a small village like this to come to terms with. And Ray being such a big personality in village life, too," Lily whispered.

"It is that," Tanya replied, "I, for one, will be glad to no longer have the police swarming all over like little ants!"

They all agreed on that, and Flora stood to refill the large teapot the four women were sharing. She knew that gossip was normal in such a rural village, and to be expected, though Flora did feel slightly uncomfortable partaking in it – she felt torn between being Adam's confidante and sharing what she knew with her friends. Not that in this case she knew anything yet. However, it still played on her mind as she added the fresh teabags and boiling water to the pot.

Just as Flora took her seat at the table again, the bell above the door tinkled to herald the arrival of someone else. Instead of an actual customer, or a local wanting information and a good gossip, it was the young woman from the cake stall at the fete.

"Hello?" she stuck her head around the door nervously, seeing only Aaron and Reggie at first, "Is Flora here at all?"

Hearing her voice, Reggie took off from the table, where he had been waddling over the pages of Aaron's book as he tried to read, and swooped over to greet the new guest, "Ooh sexy beast!" he squawked happily.

"Oh! Hello Reggie!" Emma laughed as the bird landed on her arm, just above her gloved hand.

"Come on in, Emma!" Flora said, standing, and moving to that end of the room, "how are you doing? Your table looked to have a lot of customers on Saturday!"

"Yes, it was more successful than I could possibly have hoped," Emma said, coming fully into the room and smiling at the women assembled, who were staring at her with interest, "that's why I'm here actually, that lovely older gentleman – Mr. Bentley is it? – said I should pop by to discuss the empty shop on Front Street with you."

"Of course, excuse me ladies," Flora nodded towards the other women, and indicated one of the free tables near the door to Emma.

"Can I get you a drink, Emma"

"No, thank you, it's just a flying visit to see if the shop is still available, and to confirm what my next steps should be, before I head home again."

"And where is home?" Flora asked, trying to show interest, though in truth her mind was still reeling from recent events.

"Oh! Err, over by Alnwick way," Emma replied, indicating a large town further North.

"Lovely, I haven't visited there yet."

"Well, you're welcome to come round, anytime, though I am quite busy at the moment," Emma fussed over Reggie without looking up.

"Don't worry, I'm very occupied here as well."

"I can imagine! Did you see the police in the village this morning? I noticed as I drove through!"

Flora cast a worried glance at Aaron, who was clearly listening whilst pretending to read, "Yes," she whispered, "we had a very unfortunate event here yesterday, but I will have to fill you in another time."

"Oh, I see," Emma looked curious, but didn't press the issue further. Instead she turned her attention to the matter at hand, "So, about the shop...?"

"Yes, it's yours if you want it – Get down, Reggie!" Flora spoke sternly to the parrot, who had climbed onto Emma's head and was pecking at her pretty hairband.

"Oh, he's okay," Emma giggled, suddenly appearing a lot younger than her formal attire would suggest.

"No, he has to learn," Flora said firmly, gently unhooking Reggie's claws from Emma's shiny, brown hair and letting him waddle up her own arm onto her shoulder.

"She's a cracker!" Reggie squawked in protest, but did at least stay put.

"Yes, the shop is yours if you want it, it's just small as far as I know, but I think you would make a great addition to the village," Flora smiled, "I will let Harry Bentley know to prepare the rental contract and give you his contact details."

"That's perfect, thank you," Emma replied happily, as she readjusted her floral hairband with her pretty, pink-gloved hands.

"Do you have gloves to match every outfit?" Flora asked, genuinely impressed by the younger woman's co-ordination.

"Yes," Emma laughed, slightly embarrassed, "it comes from working with loose sweets and candies, I just factor the gloves into every outfit now!"

"Well, I think they're lovely!" Flora said, standing, "I look forward to seeing your shop when it opens. Please do start fitting it out whenever you're ready. Will you be moving into the flat above as well?"

"Yes, that's the plan, I'm keen to get a taste of village life!"

"Well, for the most part, it's lovely here, you should fit right in."

"Thank you, Flora," Emma said, as Reggie swooped up and across to her shoulder where she stood by the door.

"You're my honey," he clucked, nuzzling into Emma's neck affectionately.

"You've made a friend for life," Flora laughed, as the bell tinkled above the door and Emma made her way out.

"She seems nice, I remember her from the sweetie

stall," Aaron said, his lower lip quivering.

"Oh, Aaron, come and have a hug," Flora said, extending her arms to the boy, "What's wrong?"

"I miss my mum!" he whispered against her shoulder, and Flora felt a lump appear in her throat. She wanted to speak, but was afraid that doing so would release the emotions which she was trying to hide from the boy.

"Aw laddie," thankfully the other three women came over to the rescue, with Betty leading the small group, "Your mum will be fine, you and she can come to stay with me. It'll be grand, and I can cook all your favourite meals," Betty said indulgently.

"Thank you, Granny Betty," Aaron replied, using the familiar term he had come to know her by, even though Betty wasn't his real relation.

"Yes, it is all good," Tanya added to the reassurance.

"Why don't you come to see the piglets with your mum when she's home?" Lily added, trying to distract the boy.

Aaron sniffed and rubbed his eyes, holding out his hand for Reggie. The bird was hopping from one foot to the other on Flora's shoulder, clearly picking up on the sad atmosphere. He jumped eagerly onto the boy and rubbed his hand with his head feathers.

"We're a team!" he squawked, repeating one of the phrases Flora had been trying to teach him, of his own accord for the first time.

"We are!" The women all agreed, though more than one had tears in her eyes.

ELEVEN

Lily had to leave to tend to the farm shop, but Betty and Tanya were still in the tearoom, entertaining Aaron with drawings and chatter, when the door opened and an exhausted looking Shona came in.

"Mum!" Aaron shouted, rushing to wrap his arms around her. The three women stood and waited in turn to also hug Shona, who was followed into the tearoom by Adam.

"So, I hope they have seen sense and let you go?" Betty said sternly, casting a warning glance at Bramble.

"Not exactly," Shona whispered, her eyes filling with tears. She turned away, so that Aaron wouldn't see her crying.

"It has been a long night," Adam said gently, "and Ms. Dodds has helped us with our enquiries, but I'm afraid she needs to stay in the village as we will probably need to bring her in again. Sorry, Flora, I need to dash, Blackett is waiting in the squad car," Adam looked apologetically in Flora's direction, before turning swiftly on his heels and leaving.

"Come and have a sit down and something to eat," Flora said, guiding Shona to the table the women had been using, "I could make you a bacon sandwich and a lovely pot of sweet tea?"

"I'm not really hungry," Shona whispered, before seeing her son's swollen, watery eyes, and quickly adding, "but that would be lovely, thank you, Flora."

Betty clucked and fussed around Shona, making sure she was comfortable, while Tanya helped Flora in the small kitchen area. Reggie retreated to his perch in the back of the room. He was good at picking up on undercurrents, and had clearly decided to make himself scarce.

"So," Betty said, as soon as they were all sitting down again, and Aaron had been persuaded to go and cheer Reggie up, "so lass, how do things stand?"

"Well," Shona wiped her eye, where a tear threatened

to fall anew, "they've said I may still be charged. I think I'm their main suspect because my fingerprints are all over the pie tins – they would be though, because I re-stocked the freezers in the cellar just the other day!"

"Oh, I'm sure they will take that into account," Flora said, attempting to reassure.

"But it gets worse," Shona whispered, one eye on Aaron at the back of the room, "Detective Bramble says he heard me arguing with my dad, just before he, he..," the sobbing started afresh and Tanya came from the other side of the table to put her arms around Shona's shaking shoulders.

They drank their tea in silence, the bacon sandwiches forgotten, until Shona was ready to speak again, "I told them I didn't argue with him that day, that I was upstairs with Aaron. In fact, I'd been giving my dad the silent treatment since the day before, but they won't believe me! Detective Bramble said he saw the back of my head and knows it was me. But it can't have been me! It wasn't! The first time I'd planned on speaking to my dad that day was when I found him lying there!" Shona's voice raised in pitch and volume the more distraught she became, "Please can you speak to the detective, Flora? I know he's close to you."

"Well, yes, of course, I'll tell him exactly what you've said to me," Flora promised, though her head whirred with the difficult position she was in. Could she really use her personal relationship with Adam to get the inside picture on the case? She certainly knew Shona couldn't have killed her father, the young woman surely wasn't capable of such an act. Flora felt compelled to help her clear her name, and if that meant advocating for her with the police, then that is what she would do.

Flora felt drained when everyone had finally left – Shona and Aaron off to Betty's with her. Apparently, the police had promised Shona could collect some of their belongings from the flat above the pub that afternoon, provided she was accompanied by Bramble or Blackett. Flora stroked Reggie's smooth feathers absentmindedly and ran through the details of the previous day in her head, trying to block out the vision of Ray lying there, inert on the concrete floor.

Eventually, to distract herself from Shona's plight and from the niggling – and she knew, selfish – worry, of how this would all affect her blossoming relationship with Adam Bramble, Flora locked up the tearoom. With Reggie on her shoulder, she decided to walk up the gravel driveway to the main manor house and see how the workmen were getting on with the building repairs to the internal ceiling in the study, now that a plumber had fixed the leaking water pipes in the attic above. The roofer had already called to say that he was finished that section, and would Flora like him to move onto another part of the roof, as no part of it seemed to be without missing or damaged tiles. Flora had put him off for now, wanting to get a surveyor in to assess what needed doing once these repairs made the building safe to enter once again.

For now, though, Flora intended to just see how the men were faring, what progress they had made, and perhaps to start having a look at what needed doing in the large kitchen at the back of the property. Up until the ceiling collapse, Flora had been focusing on the front rooms, and sorting the mountains of paperwork there, so she had neglected the other spaces in the huge house. The kitchen, though, she remembered from her first visit when Harry Bentley had shown her around, faced the back rose gardens and lawns, and had a glass conservatory or garden room attached off to one side. Flora thought a potter around here might lift her spirits, and enable her to focus on better, hopefully happier, times to come. Certainly, she was in desperate need of some fresh air.

Arriving at the side door to the manor which she always used – preferring this to the heavy, main door – Flora was shocked to see this standing slightly ajar. Until, however, she remembered the builder's van sitting out front on the driveway, and that she had given them a key. Looking more closely, though, Flora noticed some damage around the lock, as if someone had tried to force entry into the building. Her heart beating fast in her chest, Flora felt Reggie angle himself into her neck protectively – he had been wary of coming up here ever since that fateful day in the study with Enid – and Flora didn't blame him. She felt the need for some support and reassurance too! As Flora tentatively reached out to pull the door properly open, a large, burly figure barrelled towards her from the other side, almost sending Flora flying backwards, and Reggie with her.

"Oh, sorry sweetheart," the man grabbed Flora's elbow as she fell, hoisting her back up. By the looks of him, he was with the builder's crew, Flora thought, given the overalls and the fact he seemed to be covered in plaster and paint.

"I'm just..," Flora started to explain herself, then stopped abruptly as the man had already sauntered off in the direction of the van. Instead she simply walked into the building, where she could hear some chatting coming from the kitchen.

"Mrs. Miller! What a pleasant surprise! The lads and me are just having a quick cuppa," Ted Charlton, whose building company it was, jumped off a wobbling stool at the ancient Formica breakfast bar and came to shake Flora's hand, "and who is this handsome fella?"

"There'll be hell to pay!" Reggie shrieked nervously, sending the man skittering backwards a couple of paces.

"Don't mind Reggie here," Flora said, feeling deflated all of a sudden. Here she was, in what was supposed to be her kitchen, feeling as out of place as ever. She wondered for a moment if she would ever feel at home in this huge house, "I was just coming to see how you're getting on with the work?"

"Well, there's good news and there's bad news!"

"Oh?" Flora wasn't sure she liked the sound of that, "Tell me the good news first, then."

"Well, another day or two and we'll be finished, though I've noticed there's a lot more needs doing about the place, and I could fit you in if you want us to continue?" Ted angled hopefully for the contract to be extended.

"I'd rather get a surveyor in first, and then I'll let you know," Flora said, feeling honestly overwhelmed with the task at hand, "So, tell me the bad news."

"Morris here went out for a smoke just after we arrived and when he came back in, he says it looks like the door's been tampered with. It may have been like that when we got here, to be honest, I can't say as I didn't pay much attention to it other than to put the key in the lock."

"I saw it as I came in," Flora said, feeling her anxiety rising. Reggie had taken to doing flying swoops of the large room, clearly trying to keep all the men on their toes.

"I'd get that looked at, and maybe an extra lock put on, you can't be too careful," Ted said, kindly, rinsing his mug in the sink and gesturing for his gang to get back to work.

Flora stood silently as the four men filed past her, her brain working a mile a minute trying to think of who would want to break into this dilapidated place. At least, whoever it was, they hadn't managed to break the lock, or had thought better of it. It could be an organised burglary, but those were few and far between – pretty much unheard of – in these parts. Or just someone chancing their luck on finding a treasure. More likely, Flora thought with a sinking feeling, it was someone local with something specific in mind that they wanted to find. And Flora thought she knew exactly who that could be.

TWELVE

Flora dragged her heels as she walked along Front Street. She had dropped a reluctant Reggie off at home, having to prize his talons away from her shoulder. Clearly, he felt as unsettled as she did. This was turning into an extremely long lunch break, and Flora should have the tearoom open, but she couldn't help herself. The door to The Bun in the Oven was still covered in police tape, and Flora tried not to stare at the policeman on duty there –surrounded by bunches of flowers no doubt placed by Ray's regular customers – all the time wondering if Adam would be inside. Instead, she hurried on, past the duck pond and up behind the Green to Cook's Row, which had been changed now to Crook's Run. Unlike previously, however, this didn't bring even the smallest of smiles to Flora's lips. She rushed past the street sign and on to Phil's house. It being the last week of the school summer holidays, she expected him to be at home, even at this hour in the afternoon.

"Flora?" Phil couldn't keep the surprise from his face, "I wasn't expecting to see you here."

"I wasn't expecting to come, not after our last conversation," Flora admitted honestly, "but there's been a, ah, a development up at The Rise..," now that she was about to say it out loud, Flora was having very grave misgivings about having come here. Especially having come alone. She really should have waited and asked Adam to come with her.

"A development? With Harold's files?" Phil prompted.

They were still standing on the doorstep, and an invite inside didn't seem to be forthcoming. Flora shuffled from one foot to the other uncomfortably, "Ah, the files? No, of course not, it's a development with the door."

"The door? To the tearoom? What has that got to do with me?"

"No, not the tearoom. Actually, it's nothing, Phil, sorry I shouldn't have come."

"No, hold on!" Phil grasped her arm lightly to hold Flora in place, "I hope you're not saying what I think you're saying. Has someone been messing with the door as in trying to break in?"

"Well, now that you mention it, yes, I..," Flora pulled her arm from Phil's grasp and turned to leave.

"So, not content with accusing me of murder last month, you're now accusing me of breaking and entering and effectively calling me a thief!" Phil shouted, and Flora was glad there was no one around to hear. She winced under the volume of his onslaught.

"No, Phil, as far as I know they didn't actually manage to gain entry..," Flora knew as soon as the words left her mouth that she had said the wrong thing again, as Phil completely flew off the handle.

"Why leave it at burglary, Flora, Lady Miller of Baker's Rise, why not accuse me of Ray's murder as well and be done with it?" Phil grabbed her arm again.

"Now hold on there, lad," the calming voice of Billy Northcote came from the bottom of the garden path, and Flora was never so grateful to hear it as right then.

"Billy, how are you today?" Flora asked, turning to face the elderly gent as he walked up to where she and

Phil stood at the door. Thankfully, Phil's hand fell from her arm at the interruption.

"I'm well lass, nothing to complain about. I wanted to talk to you actually," Billy linked arms with Flora and led her away, diffusing the situation expertly. Phil was left scowling after them, though Flora didn't chance a look back at him. She could feel his eyes boring into her back and the icy atmosphere chilling her to the bone.

"Thank you so much, Billy, things were getting a bit heated. I put my foot in my mouth again, I'm afraid. When will I ever learn?" Flora questioned, more for her own benefit.

"Aye lass, I heard the last part at least, come in for a cuppa and you can tell me all about it."

After spilling her worries to Billy, without actually telling him the sensitive information pertaining to Phil's father, and hearing his wisdom that it could be anyone who had had a go at the lock, not necessarily even someone from the village, Flora felt calmer. She trudged back along Front Street and up to the tearoom, not stopping to collect Reggie as there was only an hour and a half left till closing time. As she cleaned the coffee machine of invisible dust and wiped all of the beautiful china crockery – anything to keep her hands busy and her mind distracted – Flora heard the tinkle of the shop bell behind her. It was Pepper Jones, without George, and she seemed unsure of herself as she stepped delicately over the threshold.

A small woman, with salt and pepper hair cut in a short style, her face seemed quite gaunt beneath thin-rimmed glasses.

"Pepper, it's lovely to see you!" This was the first time Pepper had ventured up to the tearoom. Indeed, Flora had been surprised to see her at both the fete and the pub the other day. When she had enquired with Betty, a few weeks after arriving, why the woman was never seen out and about much, Betty had whispered that Pepper and George's only daughter had run away about nine years before, when she was only seventeen, causing a big man hunt in the surrounding areas. For once, Betty didn't seem to know any more details, only that Pepper had retreated into her shell after that, becoming almost reclusive, except for arranging the Christmas Talent Show every year, as that had been one of her daughter's favourite events.

Flora was careful not to let her surprise show as she gave Pepper the choice of any table, all were free.

Pepper sat at the spot closest to the door, as if she might want to make her escape at any moment – at least, that was how it seemed to Flora. She fiddled with her specs and then her watch, as Flora stood poised with her notebook to take the order. After a few uncomfortable seconds, Flora sat down beside the woman and waited for her to speak.

"Flora, I was wondering if you have heard anything? In here, from customers, I mean? Or from your detective friend?" Pepper eventually asked, her throat sounding hoarse as she rushed the words out quickly.

"Heard anything?"

"About the incident… with Ray? Have they charged Shona?"

"I don't think so, Pepper, no, is there a reason why you ask?"

"No, no not at all, just neighbourly curiosity getting the better of me! Thank you," and with that, the woman stood up and rushed back out, leaving Flora rather unsettled by the visit.

Flora had just changed into a comfortable pair of slacks and a beige ribbed top, with her cosy house shoes, when the front doorbell of the coach house rang. Reggie immediately discarded the grape he was enjoying, launching it across the room as he flew straight along the narrow hallway to perch on the door handle. Flora rushed along from her bedroom, trying to flatten her hair with her hands as she hurried.

"Adam! What a lovely surprise! I wasn't sure when I would next get to see you, what with everything that's going on."

"I know, I'm sorry love, I ditched you yesterday didn't I?" Bramble pecked Flora on the cheek before he followed her to the sitting room.

"With good reason! I didn't mind. Are you hungry?"

"Starving actually," Adam's face, with its sunken eyes and heavy grey bags underneath, belied his lack of sleep the previous night, "Would you like to go out to eat?"

"No, you look shattered, let me cook you something," Flora racked her brain to try to think of what she had in that would feed two of them on such short notice. It would have to be pesto pasta and garlic bread with salad, she decided. Not original, but at least it might put some colour into Adam's cheeks.

"So, you've been busy on the case?" Flora tried to ask as nonchalantly as possible, once she had set the water to boiling for the pasta and made Adam a strong cup of coffee.

"We have, interviewing all the same people we talked to last month about Harold – well apart from the Reverend and his wife, of course," Adam grimaced, "Talking to that Doctor Edwards and his wife again wasn't pleasant, I can tell you, especially when I had to reveal what you'd seen. I didn't tell the good doctor that his wife had been propositioning Ray, of course, but the woman herself looked fit to keel over when she realised I knew."

"You didn't say it was me who saw them?"

"No, no of course not, don't worry, love. We kept that bit anonymous."

"So, is she a suspect then, Edwina?" Flora was trying so hard not to pry, and she wouldn't be offended if Adam told her to butt out.

"Well, that's confidential to the case, but I can say that we have one clear suspect in mind. After all, we know Edwina wasn't the last to argue with the deceased."

"You mean Shona?"

"Sorry, love, I can't…"

"I know, I know, sorry, it's just she's my friend, and with a young son and all," Flora felt the tears spring uninvited to her eyes. Adam must've seen it too, as he stood up from the settee and came across to her armchair, gently helping Flora to a standing position and taking her into his arms.

THIRTEEN

"I've got you, have a good cry," Adam whispered into Flora's hair, "it's been a trying time all round."

"The water will be boiling," Flora whispered against Adam's chest, as Reggie landed on her head, nuzzling close and chirping worriedly.

"It'll keep, let's just stand a minute, I could do with a cuddle," Adam admitted, causing Flora's tears to fall faster, and her arms to tighten around his waist.

They stood like that for quite a while, until Adam's rumbling stomach prompted them to break apart.

"I'll prepare the food, you sit here and put the television on for a bit," Flora said, squeezing Adam's hand once and then shuffling into her small kitchen.

Reggie followed her, "My Flora, my Flora," he squawked, and Flora couldn't tell whether he spoke from a place of possession or protection. It didn't matter to her, though, she only cared that she had his companionship.

When Flora brought the pasta bowls through twenty minutes later, thinking they could eat on their laps in front of the television, she found Adam sound asleep. Pulling the tartan throw from the back of the couch over him, Flora put Adam's bowl of food back on the counter to be reheated later, and sat down at the kitchen table with her own meal. A heavy melancholy settled over her, and she was glad of the company of her feathered friend.

The next morning dawned misty and with a distinct chill in the air. After seeing a rather sleepy Adam out after eleven the night before, Flora herself felt much like the weather – her brain fogged and her mood frosty. She hurried along the damp path to the tearoom with Reggie on her shoulder – he hadn't wanted to let her out of his sight after her emotional upheaval of the previous evening, and Flora had been comforted by it. After all that, she hadn't even managed to speak to Adam about the confrontation with Phil. Flora knew she'd made a mistake, both in going alone and in being the one to bring up the topic with the schoolteacher. Today, she intended to rectify that by phoning Pat Hughes first thing to report the damage to the door. Annoyed with herself, that in the previous day's turmoil she had forgotten to get a locksmith to change the lock on the side door of the manor house and to add another couple for extra security, Flora decided to make that her top priority after speaking with Pat. Although she was trying to give herself a little grace, what with the shock of the murder and the predicament Shona now found herself in, Flora was still annoyed that she had overlooked this.

Pat had answered on the first ring and, to Flora's distinct surprise, he was the epitome of professionalism, saying he would go immediately up to The Rise and take a look, and then report back to her. Flora had felt reassured by the conversation and, managing to also get hold of a local locksmith on the first try, arranged for the door to be sorted that afternoon, giving Pat a chance to look at it first. All in all, it had gone more smoothly that Flora had hoped, and she sat down with what she felt was a well-earned cup of coffee, making a note in the diary on her phone to also get some quotes to have security cameras fitted around the main building of the manor house.

As the bell tinkled above the door at that exact moment, Flora swallowed down the sigh which rose to her lips, telling herself that customers were what she wanted, needed even, in the tearoom. Thankfully, it was the normally cheery face of Will Monkhouse which greeted her as she stood and turned to welcome her first customer of the day. His smile seemed forced this morning, though, and when Flora looked more closely she saw the tell-tale lines of worry across Will's forehead and around his tired eyes.

"Not the Vet! Not the Vet!" Reggie's panicked squawks rang out, despite Will going over to rub the bird on the head. Reggie took off before Will's fingers had made contact, however, heading to take cover behind the counter. He had never done that before, and Flora found herself quite bemused by his actions.

"Reggie, Reggie, it's not safe there," Flora said, as she saw his green wing peeking out, "there are hot machines!" Flora eyed the huge coffee monster with distrust – despite Tanya's efforts at teaching her, Flora had never quite got the hang of the machine when she was alone.

"Not safe, not safe," Reggie repeated, but refused to budge until Flora went across, bent down and picked him up, tucking him inside the open flap of her cardigan.

"There. Sorry about that, Will, what can I get you?" The man in question had taken a seat at the table nearest the counter, and was currently raking his hands through his shaggy hair in distress. Flora's heart went out to him as she took the seat opposite.

"Ah, I'm not really in the mood for any cake today, Flora, sorry, it was you I was looking for actually."

"Of course, I could get you some sweet tea, that might help?" Flora replied gently.

"Thank you, yes, that would be fine," Will said, sitting up a bit straighter and making eye contact for the first time, "it has been a difficult few days."

"That's an understatement," Flora agreed, adding boiling water and a teabag to a pretty teapot and bringing it across to the table, "how is Shona?"

"As well as can be expected, I spoke to her this morning, she and Aaron had a comfortable night at Betty's so that's something."

"It is, I know Betty will fuss over them and make sure they feel at home. How about you? How are you holding up?"

Will took a moment to compose himself before he answered. A sheen of moisture covered his eyes, and Flora busied herself pouring the tea into a china cup which already sat on the table, to give him a moment of privacy. Then she picked up her own cup of coffee, which was beginning to cool from earlier.

"Well, it's been… very hard, Flora, very challenging indeed," Will's voice faltered and Flora put her hand on his arm in a gesture of comfort, waiting patiently until he spoke again, "I know Shona wouldn't have… couldn't have done something like that. It's not in her nature. Besides, she loved the man, in spite of his faults! He took her in when her mum kicked her out and she was pregnant with Aaron. I just need to know what to do to help her. To clear her name. They were meant to be spending Sunday afternoon with me, her and Aaron, but I was called out on an emergency at Drake's farm over Witherham way. Didn't get back till the evening. There was no signal up there, so by the time I checked my phone I had seven missed messages and a dozen texts, only one from Shona, and the rest from concerned villagers… She should have been with me that day, nowhere near the pub at all!"

"Oh, I'm sorry, that's an awful way to find out, Will, and you shouldn't blame yourself for being out on a work call," Flora tried to console him, though she knew there were no words that would make the situation better right now.

"I'm not important, and I'm so grateful to you for taking Aaron for the night, I just need to know how to help Shona. Has your detective friend said anything?" The hope in his eyes cut through Flora, and she desperately wished she had some information that would comfort the man. Sadly, she had nothing.

"I'm so sorry, Will. Detective Bramble is careful what he tells me, for confidentiality reasons, you know? Apart from that, I haven't heard anything that would help Shona...Though I'm convinced she's innocent and I'm going to do all I can to help her prove it," Flora added, when Will's face dropped again at her reply.

"It's okay, I knew it was a long shot," Will's chair scraped back as he hurried to leave, his cup of tea left untouched on the table.

Flora felt sick and shaky as she bade him goodbye, wishing with all her heart that she had been able to offer something positive to help the situation. Instead, all she seemed to be able to provide were cups of tea and a sympathetic, listening ear.

FOURTEEN

It was the Tuesday of the following week, the first week in September, that most of the residents of Baker's Rise village gathered in the church beside the Green to mourn the passing of Ray Dodds. Schoolchildren had returned back to their normal routines the previous day, following their summer break, so the village already seemed quieter than it had all season. Flora and Betty walked alongside Harry, behind Will, Shona and Aaron who led the sombre funeral procession which was following the coffin-laden hearse through the village. Behind Flora, Tanya walked arm-in arm with Pat, in a spectacularly large hat adorned with striking black feathers. Apparently distinctly disgruntled to be relegated further back in the procession, Doctor and Mrs. Edwards walked with backs ram-rod straight, about a foot apart from each other. Behind them, George and Pepper Jones followed with Billy Northcote, just in front of Lily and Stan Houghton, leading a whole crowd of people whom Flora didn't recognise but who she assumed were relatives of Ray and other locals.

The hearse came to a stop at the bottom of the footpath which led up to the old, stone church. Casting a quick glance back through the group, Flora was relieved to not see Phil amongst the gathering – presumably he was busy teaching the new term. She did manage to unwittingly catch Joe Stanton's eye, though, and earned herself a fierce glare in return, so Flora quickly turned to face the front again. Shona stood in stoic silence in front of her, dressed all in the black of mourning, with Will's arm around her waist, and her own arm around Aaron's shoulders. When she herself turned to see the crowd amassed behind them, Flora was shocked by the change that had overcome the young woman in the short time since her father's murder. Her once-rounded, bonnie cheeks were now thin and taut, her smooth skin now succumbed to worry lines. Shona's face was white and her eyes haunted. Flora knew that she had been called in for questioning on at least one more occasion since that first day, but had again been let out without charge. So far, the evidence was all circumstantial it would seem.

Flora got the impression that the police were hoping a witness would materialise to confirm Shona's guilt. They had again interviewed everyone – Flora included – who had been in the pub that afternoon, in the hope that someone had gone to use the bathroom and seen the culmination of the argument of which Adam had witnessed a part. Presumably, that line of enquiry had come up empty, as Shona had not been brought back in to the station – not yet anyway.

"Flora, lass" Betty's quick whisper brought Flora back from her musings, as she realised the coffin and wreaths had been unloaded and the procession was once again on the move towards the church doors. Reverend Marshall waited to welcome the mourners, his face a picture of sadness on this day, as everyone filed in and found a pew. Flora pitied the kind man, that his first official engagement in the village should be a funeral – and of a local man murdered, at that.

Once seated, Betty swivelled around next to Flora on the second row back from the front, her sharp eyes assessing the group which was still filling up the church behind them.

"I wonder which of his wives will be here? I haven't heard hide nor hair of the first two for decades, so I doubt they even know or care but... oh! There's Gloria who you saw at the fete, with those two lumps of lard for sons! No sign of Shona's Mum, Wendy, though, and I heard the last one, Patricia, passed away recently. Maybe the daughter will come, Amelia her name was… Oh, there's Lily and Stan come down from the farm!" Betty gave what could only be described as a running commentary, in somewhat of a stage whisper, until Flora nudged her to indicate the service was about to begin.

It had been a difficult and draining day, with the wake being held in the tiny church hall which backed onto the main church building. Betty and Lily had done most of the catering for Shona, with George and Pepper providing extra baked goods, and Flora supplying and serving the teas and coffees with Tanya. It was mainly the locals who stopped by after the service, with Gloria – the only one of Ray's exes who had showed up – and her sons leaving straight away. Flora was glad of it, she didn't think Shona could handle any confrontation. There had been quite a few faces in the congregation which neither Lily nor Betty recognised, and there was much speculation at the wake as to whether any of those could be more of Ray's errant offspring. Will had quickly ushered Shona out into the church garden, ostensibly for some fresh air, but Flora suspected it was to get her away from any gossip. They made such a sweet couple, and Flora hoped that their relationship would survive this tragic time.

Seeing them together made her think of Adam, whom she had seen only once in the past week, and even then only briefly when he called into the tearoom. It was Blackett who had turned up to interview her again, which Flora understood, given Adam's compromised position where she was concerned. Nevertheless, Flora was embarrassed to acknowledge to herself that she had sat up till half past ten each night waiting to see if Adam would call by, going to bed disappointed each time when he did not. Annoyed with herself, she rubbed the plate she was holding a little too hard in the sink and the whole thing cracked in two.

"Drat!" Flora muttered, putting the pieces into the bin, and rubbing her hand where the sharp edge of the broken crockery had grazed her palm.

"Let me see," Harry said, turning from the draining board where he was drying the dishes as she washed them.

"It's nothing, I just..," Flora was mortified to realise that there were tears running down her face.

"Aw lass," Harry rubbed her back uncomfortably, until Betty swooped in from the doorway and enveloped Flora in a huge hug.

"There now, it's been a difficult time," Betty whispered, "come and take the weight off your feet."

"I'm fine really, I'm so sorry," Flora said, rubbing her sleeve across her eyes and nose indelicately.

"We can finish here, lass, you be getting off. You've left that bird a long time as it is," Harry said kindly.

"I have that," Flora grasped onto the offered excuse gratefully, as she grabbed her coat and bag from the back of the door. She hastily removed the old apron she had borrowed from the church kitchen, to cover the smart black dress she wore, and left with a quick kiss for Betty and Harry. She would call to see Shona the next day, as she and Aaron were still staying at Betty's. Flora assumed the young woman would want some space this evening, just as she herself did.

Curled up on the sofa in her favourite plaid pyjamas, with a cup of chamomile tea in one hand and a parrot on the other, Flora finally let out the huge breath it felt like she had been holding all day. It was only half past seven in the evening, but Flora had every intention of finishing her drink and then heading to bed with her latest online purchase – a how-to book on writing stories for young children. Not that Flora thought she would do much reading tonight, she'd probably be out like a light as soon as her head hit the pillow! As it was, she had almost fallen asleep in the lingering bubble bath she'd taken straight after getting home from the funeral.

Sat under the wool throw on the sofa, warm from her tea, and with Reggie snuggled on her shoulder, leaning against her neck, Flora was just beginning to doze off when her phone buzzed. Imagining it would be either the emailed invoice from the builders, who had finished up in the manor house the previous week on schedule, or a message from the architectural surveyor who Flora had contacted to give the building a good look-over, she was tempted to not check till morning. Something prompted Flora to pick her phone up, however – probably the curiosity which so often got her into trouble – and she was surprised to see a text from Adam asking her if it was too late to pop round. Considering for a moment her current state, wearing her nightclothes, and with her hair scraped back in a bun, Flora considered saying no, but her desire to see him far outweighed her appearance. So, five minutes later, she heard his car pull up outside.

"Now Reggie, be good," Flora warned, as the bird was very grumpy at being woken from his slumber.

"Be good! Be good!" the bird repeated in a tone that implied he was the one telling Flora off!

"Flora, I'm sorry to disturb you so late, but I was just in the village and…" Adam trailed off, smiling ruefully, "I needed to see you, that's all."

"Of course, it's only, what? Eight o'clock? Come on in."

"Were you sleeping?" Adam eyed her dishevelled state warily and kissed Flora apologetically on the cheek.

"Just dozing. It's been a long day."

" I can imagine. I really wanted to come to the funeral to be there for you, but it wouldn't have been approp…"

Flora cut him off. She didn't want to go through the whole day in her head again, "I know. I understood. Don't worry."

As Flora made more tea for them both – even Adam admitted it was a bit late for the strong coffee he always chose – she wondered aloud what he had been doing in the village at this time of day.

"Well, I can't say much, but there's been a development in the case."

"Really? Today?"

"Yes, after the funeral someone came forward."

"To implicate Shona or to absolve her?" Flora needed to know.

"Sorry, love, I shouldn't have come round…I can't say anything more, I've already said too much, I…" Adam shoved his hands in his jacket pockets and his eyes strayed to the door. Clearly he was wishing he hadn't visited.

Flora silently chastised herself for giving a good impression of a nagging fishwife, and hoped to smooth things over, "Adam, sorry, can we start again? How about we rewind the last five minutes so we don't mention the case?"

Adam looked visibly more relaxed as he held out his arms for Flora to walk into his embrace, "That would be great, love, thank you, I just need some down-time with my best friend, that's all."

Her face heating from the knowledge he considered her his best friend, and her body enjoying the warmth of being in his arms, Flora simply nodded against

Adam's chest. That was exactly what she needed, too. Even just for a moment, she wanted to forget the storm of stress and suspicion that they were in, and just pretend they were a normal couple, taking things slowly and enjoying each other's company.

FIFTEEN

In the end, given that Flora could barely keep her eyes open, Adam had only stayed for an hour, but it had been so nice to feel his gentle kiss on her lips and to have his good company, that Flora had been glad of the brief time they'd shared together. No doubt when this was all over, they would have more time to be together, and could go out openly again without being under the scrutiny of the whole village. The early September day was warm, so Flora opted to wear one of her floaty summer dresses, assuming it would probably be one of her last chances to do so this year. Her hair had taken much longer than usual to tame, having become slightly damp in the bath the previous evening and then spent the night in a messy bun. Flora made a mental note to pop into Baker's Rise Cuts and Dyes later that day to make an appointment with Amy.

Surprised that there were no baked goods as yet, given that George Jones had not missed a day so far, Flora busied herself placing fresh china cups and saucers carefully on the tables. There were some teacakes and a small chocolate cake left over from his last delivery, but if George didn't arrive soon she would have to try out the only recipe she knew – scones. Lily had been planning to move on to giving Flora fruit pie lessons before Ray's unfortunate end, and now neither of the women could quite face it.

Flora's mind kept returning to what Adam had said the night before about a development in the case. She hoped to goodness that it would work out in Shona's favour this time, but what it could be, Flora didn't want to speculate. She certainly wasn't going to mention it to Shona and Betty, in case it got their hopes up and also because if Adam found out, then he'd be even less likely to tell her things in future. *No*, Flora decided, *best to keep it to herself*. Deep in her thoughts, she barely heard the bell above the door, and it was Reggie who alerted Flora to her customer.

"She's a corker! She's a corker!" Reggie shrieked happily, flapping above Tanya so that she could barely get through the door.

"Desist, silly bird!" Tanya said firmly, though she

smiled as she did so. Just to prove she hadn't ruffled his feathers, Reggie landed on Tanya's shoulder and waddled up to her neck, chirping happily.

"Good bird," she conceded, before finally addressing Flora, "So, are you still on for Jazzercise tonight?"

"I, ah, well, I..," in truth Flora had forgotten about the weekly event, which, although it was getting easier, still left her aching for the rest of the week. She tried in vain to think up an excuse on the spot, but Tanya was way ahead of her.

"It will do you good, to take your mind off everything," Tanya said, a small smile of victory already forming.

"Oh, okay then," Flora smiled back in resignation and said, "time for a quick coffee?"

Before Tanya could answer, the door to the tearoom flew open and Pepper Jones stood there, framed with the sunlight behind her, her short hair sticking out at all angles and her eyes wild.

"Pepper?" Flora asked tentatively, moving slowly so as not to startle her, while Tanya nipped behind the counter to put the kettle on for a cup of rejuvenating tea.

"Flora, thank goodness!" the woman launched herself into Flora's arms in a flurry of tears, and it was all Flora could do to support her weight, until Tanya came to help her get Pepper seated at the table nearest the door. For once, even Reggie had been stunned into silence by the nature of the arrival, and returned to his perch before flattening his wings down by his sides, as if making himself as small as possible to not be noticed.

"It's George," Pepper said finally, once she had caught her breath. Evidently she had run up the hill from the village.

"George? Is he ill?" Flora asked, wondering if Pepper shouldn't have instead called an ambulance and stayed with the man.

"Ill? In the head, maybe!" Pepper said, before shaking her head and adding," sorry, I didn't mean that. All I meant to say is… well, he's admitted to it!"

"To what, Pepper?" though Flora finally had an idea she knew what was coming.

"The murder! He told the police yesterday afternoon that he's the one that killed Ray!"

"No!" Tanya and Flora said in unison.

"Maybe it would help to start from the beginning," Flora suggested, as she scooped a huge spoonful of sugar into the tea before placing the full cup in front of the shaken Pepper. *Hopefully*, she thought, *the sweetness will calm her nerves.*

Tanya took the seat on the other side of Pepper and each woman held one of her hands.

"Well, you know we were in the pub the day of Ray's death," Pepper began with a statement. Both women nodded, and Flora quickly tried to rack her brain to remember if she had seen either Pepper or George leave their table in the pub that afternoon. Of course, since she herself had visited the bathroom, and then had her mind on other things, she couldn't be sure anyway.

Pepper paused, seemingly deeply distracted with worry once again. Flora squeezed her hand lightly, "Take your time, Pepper."

"Yes, well, he's gone and admitted to a murder he didn't do!" Pepper almost shrieked, causing Reggie to bury his head sideways into his wing feathers.

"Are you sure he's admitted to it?" Flora asked softly.

"Are you sure he didn't do it?" Tanya posed the

question at the exact same moment.

"Yes and yes!" Pepper was in a complete state now, and Flora wondered if they should perhaps call Dr. Edwards.

"Okay, so George is innocent but he has told the police he committed the crime," Flora clarified.

"Exactly," Pepper took a long, deep breath before continuing, "we got home after the funeral yesterday and George seemed on edge. He hasn't been himself since the Sunday Ray died. When I asked what was wrong he said he needed to make a phone call. The next I knew, the two detectives had arrived and after they'd questioned George they took him away to the station."

"What did he tell them, could you hear?" Tanya asked.

"I wasn't in the room, but I may have been standing very close to the sitting room door, if you know what I mean," Pepper admitted, "He told them that he did it, that he was angry about Ray using a new pie supplier. That was it, they took him away! He must've been at the station all night, unless he's already in prison!" Pepper began sobbing again.

"Okay, let's take a minute," Flora said, holding the cup

of tea up for Pepper to drink from, as the woman's own hands were shaking too much, "then we can think about it all more clearly."

"You are sure he didn't do it?" Tanya asked, when they had all had a few sips of their tea, earning her a glare from Flora.

Pepper was more composed now, and spoke clearly, "Well, I popped home from the pub, just for five minutes, on that Sunday, to check I'd turned the oven off after Sunday lunch, so I wasn't with George the whole time. When I got back the entire room was sitting in eerie silence, and as I slipped back into my seat, George whispered that something had happened to Ray."

"Just out of interest, Pepper, did you use the main front doors of the pub or the back door?" Flora asked, her mind whirring.

"The front door, both times. It was after I returned that the police locked it so no one could enter or leave the building."

"So, if we assume George is innocent, then he must be covering for someone. Is it Shona do you think?" Flora asked.

"No, I'm pretty sure it's me," Pepper said, a sense of defeat now washing over her. The atmosphere in the room could be cut with a knife.

Tentatively, Flora asked, "And does he have good reason to cover for you, Pepper?"

All eyes were on the woman now, including those of a certain feathered friend who had his head cocked and was listening intently.

SIXTEEN

"I didn't kill Ray Dodds!" Pepper's voice rose in indignation now, "but I do know why George would think I may have done it," she whispered the last words.

"I am a bit confused," Tanya said, standing to turn on the big coffee machine, "I need more caffeine, I think!"

Flora rubbed Pepper's arm gently, taking a moment to gather her thoughts, until Tanya was once again sat with them, "Okay, tell us why George might think you committed murder," Flora said kindly.

Pepper took a deep breath before she began, wiping her wet eyes on one of the pretty napkins which were placed carefully on each doily-covered table, "So, you may know that George and I have one daughter, Anna.

She's the same age as Shona, I think, though she had left the village before Shona returned. It was the talk of the Baker's Rise gossip machine when Anna ran away. She was only sixteen, you see, and the light of our lives. After she left, my whole world crumbled. George threw himself into his bakery, and I stayed at home."

"Why did she leave, if you don't mind me asking?" Tanya queried gently.

"Well, that's the thing. We didn't find out until Anna made contact a couple of months ago. We had no idea why she would take off like that. She had seemed withdrawn in the months before, but we put it down to being a hormonal teenager. Of course, we searched for her for all these years, even hired a private detective in the beginning. They traced her to Edinburgh but never found her. Anyway, out of the blue in July, I got a phone call from an unknown number and it was her! My Anna! Calling to tell me she was alive and well, twenty-six now and living in Aberdeen with a husband and a baby girl!"

"You must be thrilled," Flora smiled widely, though inside she was wondering where the story was going.

"I was, of course, but I needed to know why she had gone and why she felt she couldn't come back or make contact until now. Why did we have to go through all that?"

"Did she tell you?" Tanya asked, blunt as ever.

"Not everything, just that someone in the village, a man – much older than her – had made moves on her. That he had been persistent, following her, sending messages and gifts. She was scared. Then one day, he tried rather insistently to get close to her and she ran away. Panicked. It all became too much. But I don't know why she didn't come to me. Was I that bad of a mother? I was always there for her after school, never distant…" Fat tears rolled down Pepper's face silently now. Flora pulled her into a sideways hug.

"Was that man Ray?" Tanya ventured.

Pepper nodded, "I think so. Who else could it have been?" It crossed Flora's mind that it could have been Harold, but she said nothing.

"So, she made contact…" Tanya prompted.

"Yes, she wanted us to know we had a granddaughter, and she invited us up to Scotland for Christmas. I'm thrilled, of course, and so is George, and it's given me the impetus to get out and about in village life again, but it doesn't take away a decade of pain and heartbreak. Someone needs to pay for that!"

"Did you say as much to George?"

"Yes, hence why he thinks I murdered Ray! He must think that instead of popping home I went round the back of the pub and slipped in that way!"

"I see," Flora stood up to stretch her legs and have a moment to think. She walked over to Reggie – who was pretending to be asleep, but kept opening one eye to look at them – and stroked his downy soft head feathers.

"So," Tanya said, "perhaps we should tell all of this to the police and get George out of there, yes?"

"But then they'll arrest me!" Pepper sobbed.

"Not necessarily," Flora said, "did anyone see you go home to check the oven? A neighbour maybe? We could find out. Until then, though, Tanya is right, we should phone Detective Bramble."

"I was hoping, since you and he are close, that you could make him release George without me having to go into all this?" Pepper looked up at Flora beseechingly through watery, swollen eyes.

"I'm so sorry, Pepper, our relationship is still in the very early stages, and even if it weren't he keeps his professional life very separate, as he should." Flora felt awful having to refuse.

Thankfully, in the awkward silence which ensued, the three women were distracted by a vehicle pulling up outside. Peeking through the window, Flora's stomach dropped when she saw it was Detective Blackett's car and not Adam's.

"Ladies," Blackett said by way of greeting as he entered the tearoom. The uniformed officer with him waited just outside the door, Flora noticed. *What did they expect? That Pepper would try to sprint away?*

"Hide it all! Hide it all!" Reggie said, making everything seem much worse.

"Detective Blackett, what can we do for you?" Flora asked, trying to keep her voice calm and even, whilst casting warning glances at the bird.

"It is Mrs. Jones I need to speak to, thank you, we were told by someone in the village that they had seen her heading this way," Blackett said, fixing his piercing glare on Pepper, who visibly quivered in her seat.

"Where is my George?" she whispered through chattering teeth. Flora thought that maybe a mild shock was setting in on the poor woman now.

"We have released him without charge, with a warning for wasting police time," Blackett spoke harshly, "but we need to speak to you, Mrs. Jones. We suspect he is covering for someone, and you would be the obvious suspect."

"But I didn't kill anyone!" Pepper wailed.

"It is just some questions, at this stage, but you will need to accompany us to the station," Blackett said, unwavering in his mission.

"Can I come with her?" Flora asked.

"I'm afraid not, Mrs. Miller," and with that he led a shaking Pepper through the door and out to his car.

"This is not good, not good at all," Tanya whispered, and Flora nodded her head in agreement, watching as the black saloon drove off down the gravel driveway.

SEVENTEEN

Flora wasn't sure whether she should call Adam or not. In the end, concern for poor Pepper won out and, after waving goodbye to a worried Tanya, she dialled his number on her mobile phone. It rang five times and then went to voicemail, so Flora decided to close the tearoom for a bit and take a walk up to the manor house, hoping the fresh air would help to clear her head of the tension headache that had been brewing all morning. When the builders had finished the ceiling in the study the previous week, Flora had taken advantage of their big rubbish skip and asked the men to help her throw the ancient and rusting kitchen appliances and utensils away. The skip itself was towed away the next day, leaving Flora with an empty kitchen – something which filled her with joy. She had booked a professional cleaning company to do a deep clean and was desperate to see the fruits of their labour. It would be the first room in The Rise that she could really start to see as hers, and Flora hoped it would lift her spirits this day.

It was as she had envisioned – although the counter tops were old, they sparkled and shone, as did the huge windows which looked out over the rose garden and lawns beyond. Once it was painted a cheery yellow, with new blinds and furnishings, it would be perfect. It was as she stood staring out, deep in thought once again, that Flora caught sight of Billy Northcote waving at her from the bench in the rose garden. Flora smiled, happy to spot her friend, and went out to speak with him.

"Billy! This is a lovely surprise!"

"Aye, I hope you don't mind me coming up here lass, when I'm not working, like."

"Of course not, come whenever you want!"

"Thank you greatly. It's just that I might not have that long left to smell the roses before I'm pushing up the daisies, if you know what I mean."

Flora did know what he meant, and it was a sobering thought indeed. She attempted to change the subject to something less morose, "Sorry, Billy, I'll have to remember to bring a kettle up here, then next time we can have a cuppa with our natter!"

"No worries lass," Billy reached down to the ground beside the bench and produced a thermos flask of hot tea, before pouring it into two plastic cups which hid under the lid, "there you go!"

"Oh, thank you! You're well prepared," Flora smiled.

"You have to be at my age, especially when the chill of Autumn starts creeping in!"

"I can imagine," Flora shuddered, thinking of how her own bones creaked and groaned in the mornings now.

"I was wanting to speak to you, anyway," Billy began, the smile leaving his weathered face, "about that Stanton lad."

"Joe Stanton? The one who used to be village postman?" A chill ran down Flora's spine.

"That's the one. Well, I was up here on Monday, late afternoon, and I see him skulking about the side of the house, looking all shifty like. I ask him what he's doing and he starts questioning me on what keys I have for the building. Of course, I didn't tell him I have one for that side door, that Harold gave me, but I think he suspected. Anyway, thought you should know. Mind you, I see you've got some new locks on there now, so should all be fine. Strange man that one, always gives the impression he's up to no good."

"Doesn't he just," Flora said thoughtfully, "make sure you remind me to get you copies of the new keys, I hadn't thought of that when I had the extra locks put on," she added, distracted.

They sat in companiable silence, until Flora thanked Billy for the tea and went back into the big house. She had left her mobile on the bench there, and when she checked it Flora noticed two missed calls from Adam, then a text saying he was at the tearoom and asking where she was. Flora replied quickly that if he had time he could meet her up at the manor house, and then took a seat on one of only two remaining breakfast stools – the only two that had all their legs! Flora intended to replace them when she had a new kitchen fitted, but had left them for now so she had somewhere to sit to enjoy the view. The new kitchen would have to wait until she'd had the rewiring done on the electrics.

Less than five minutes later, Flora heard Adam's car coming up the driveway which led from the Tearoom on the Rise further up the hill to the manor house itself. She hurried out to meet him, keen to see his face and desperate for a bit of reassurance.

"Hello, love," Adam said as he unbent himself from the driver's side. Flora was glad to find he was alone.

"Adam, I can't tell you how happy I am to see you!" Flora flung her arms around his neck dramatically, which was unlike her, and Adam staggered back slightly under the force.

"Hey, sweetheart, what's happened?" Adam kissed her lightly on the forehead before moving Flora to arm's length so that he could see her face.

"Well, it's already been quite a day, and it's only lunch time," Flora tried hard to hold back the tears. As they walked into the house she filled Adam in on Pepper's visit to the tearoom, on the previous attempted break-in at The Rise and on what Billy had told her just now about Joe Stanton.

"You should've told me about the lock."

"I know, but you're so busy with the case, and the newly-efficient Pat Hughes has it all in hand, I think."

"Okay. Good. Well," Adam began, as he perched perilously on a breakfast stool, and Flora prayed it would take his weight, "as far as George Jones goes, I can tell you that we knew straight away he wasn't our man."

"Really? How?"

"Killer was left-handed. George favours his right."

"Oh, I see, so why keep him in all night?"

"To find out what he does know and who he's covering for. In the end, he caved and told us he thought his wife may've done it. So, now Blackett needs to interview her."

"I know, he collected her from the tearoom. Poor woman. She's adamant she's innocent though."

"Well, between you and me, I don't think she did it," Adam's voice was a low whisper, though even that seemed loud in the silence of the large, empty room.

"Do you mean you still think it was Shona?"

"That's not for me to say at present, though I can tell you that the reading of the will is tomorrow, so we may know more then as regards motive."

Flora didn't like the sound of that. Not at all. It all

sounded so cut and dried, so procedural, without even a hint that it was a young woman's future at stake. She knew that Adam couldn't help it – the detached, formal tone came with the job after all – but it didn't mean she was comfortable with it. Especially, when the young woman in question was one of Flora's friends.

She changed the subject to Joe instead, "I've an awful feeling he may have been the one trying to get into the house. After I blamed Phil as well. What a mess! But why would he do that?"

"To get something to hold against you because he sees you as the reason he lost his job? To find Harold's files so that he could take up the blackmailing where Harold left off? He was the one to deliver the letters after all, so he clearly knew about it," Adam's naturally suspicious mind seemed to work in a way that Flora's did not.

"I hadn't thought of it like that. That's not good. Not good at all," Flora muttered the last part to herself. Adam came to stand in front of her and reached out. Flora didn't need to be asked twice, she leaned forwards on her seat and wrapped her arms around his waist, laying her head on Bramble's shoulder.

"Don't fret, I won't let anything happen to you," Adam whispered, tipping Flora's quivering chin up and giving her a small peck on the lips.

"I know, I'm just… it's just one thing after another, isn't it? Since I moved in. Maybe I'm not meant to be here."

"What? Of course you are! Look at the difference you've made to this kitchen even, and of course to the village by adding a tearoom. Everyone loves you."

"Not Joe Stanton."

"Everyone who matters, I meant," Adam said, looking Flora directly in the eyes. They had never declared any strong feelings for each other, certainly not love, it was too early days for anything like that, but Flora took a moment to enjoy the knowledge that maybe, just maybe, that was what he had been hinting at.

"I'm so sorry, I have to get back to it. I can speak to Joe, and Phil too, if you like? Shall I drive you down to the tearoom?"

"Don't worry about the lock thing, you just focus on clearing Shona. Thanks, Reggie's probably chewed through a curtain by now!"

"Ha, well it's a good job I'm not the jealous type, as that bird would certainly be competition for your affection!"

126

Flora blushed and took a while to make sure all three of the new locks on the side door had clicked into place, whilst Adam waited patiently beside her. They waved goodbye to Billy, then Adam took Flora's hand in his and they walked to his car together, as if neither had anything else to think about apart from the other.

EIGHTEEN

The afternoon took a turn for the better, when Flora had a new customer in the tearoom – a lady from Alnwick who was passing through the village after visiting a client. Reggie took an immediate liking to her, and strutted proudly across her table as she ordered.

"I'm so sorry," Flora apologised, "he has no sense of space or propriety!"

"Oh, please don't apologise, he's gorgeous. Animals are my bread and butter anyway, so I'm used to most of their exhibitionist ways!" Both women chuckled and the customer introduced herself as Lizzie.

"What work do you do?" Flora was intrigued.

"I'm a pet portrait painter, actually, you wouldn't believe the number of people who want artwork of their pet, immortalised for all eternity on canvas!"

"Really?" Flora's mind began doing its whirring, where she was trying to think of too many things at once. Her first children's story sat almost finished on the typewriter in the coach house and she had the plots for at least half a dozen more in her head already. With Reggie being the main star, would it hurt to get him booked in for a portrait now? It would certainly help publicity for her books. Flora knew she was getting much too far ahead of herself, but the excitement she felt was so foreign to her recent feelings of worry and stress, that she basked in it for a moment.

"Yes, you wouldn't be interested in getting a painting of this gorgeous chap would you? I don't get to do many birds."

"It's funny you should mention that..," Flora explained about the stories as she made Lizzie's order of a cappuccino and some chocolate cake. With George still running behind, understandably so, Flora made a mental note to pop up to the farm shop for some of Lily's beautiful scones, lemon sponge loaves and banana bread to top up her current meagre offering.

Reggie, meanwhile, lapped up the attention, "You're a

corker!" he squawked happily, rubbing his head on Lizzie's palm and turning on all the charm.

So it was arranged that Flora would visit Lizzie's studio the following Monday with Reggie, to have a preliminary sketch done and some photographs taken of the bird. Seemingly attuned to the fact the two women were talking about him, Reggie chirped and waddled around the table, hopping from hand to shoulder on both women, and generally acting like he owned the place.

"Don't you be getting used to all this attention, Buster!" Flora joked.

"Pipe down!" Reggie replied, using one of Flora's regular phrases for the first time and turning it back on her.

Lizzie laughed, and Flora felt herself blushing. All in all, it was such a much-needed, positive interlude to her week.

After closing the tearoom at four o'clock and taking Reggie back home, Flora hurried down to Front Street to see if Amy could fit her in for a quick cut and blow dry. Annoyed with herself, she remembered when she got there that most of the shops in the village kept to the quaint, old-fashioned tradition of closing on a Wednesday afternoon. However, Flora felt suddenly buoyed when it struck her that it was for the best anyway as she would be getting horribly sweaty at Jazzercise later, so a new hairdo wouldn't have been well timed! Her lacklustre locks would have to survive another day or two!

The hairdressers, along with the clothes shop and the pharmacy were all in darkness. In fact, the only light came from the building slightly further along towards the Green, which Flora knew to be Emma's new sweet shop, 'Baker's Rise Candy Surprise.' Thinking she might as well pop in and say hello, Flora hurried down the street, and poked her head around the door which stood open.

"Hello? Is anybody here?"

"In the back!"

Flora followed the sound of Emma's voice to the small back room which consisted of a tiny kitchenette, a separate WC, and also contained the stairs up to the flat above.

"Emma, I'm just…" Flora stopped short when she saw not just Emma but also the man with her – Joe Stanton.

Dressed as a handyman, with a tool belt around his waist and baby pink paint splattered in his hair, Joe scowled when he saw her.

"Of course," Emma was all smiles, though from the atmosphere Flora got the impression she was interrupting something rather amorous.

"I was just passing and thought I'd see how you're getting along… just a flying visit," Flora said, directing her gaze at Emma and refusing to look at Joe. Her gut told her to make a quick exit, and Flora didn't disagree.

"Well, with Joe here helping me with the refit, I'm making great progress," Emma said, smiling at the man in question, "I've already moved my things in upstairs as Harry Bentley said it was okay to go ahead with everything even though we're not signing the contract till tomorrow – I hope that's okay?"

"Of course, that's fine. I'm glad you're getting settled so quickly and have… found help," Flora stumbled over the words.

"Well, I had a lot of time on my hands," Joe butted in pointedly.

Flora didn't acknowledge his comment, simply nodded at Emma and started backing out of the space, which felt suffocating right now. The smell of fresh paint, mixed with her own nerves, was making Flora's stomach object. Just as she turned around in the shop, though, Flora came face to face with Betty, who had clearly also seen the light on and couldn't help a quick nosey.

"Betty! Thank goodness... I mean, how nice to see you!" Flora once again tripped over the words, so happy was she to see a reassuring face.

"Aye lass, I thought I'd see what's going on."

Emma came out from the back room, thankfully leaving Joe behind, and held out her hand to Betty, "I don't think we've been properly introduced, though I do believe I saw you at the fete and perhaps in the tearoom. Emma Blenkinsopp, pleased to meet you," Emma smiled and held out her hand.

Betty shook it, but her mind was clearly elsewhere, "Blenkinsopp. Blenkinsopp. Good old Northumberland surname that. Don't hear it very often now though, can't remember the last time I heard it," Betty chewed her cheek thoughtfully.

"Well, yes, so do you have a sweet tooth?" Emma asked.

"What? Oh, I don't mind a bit of chocolate now and then, but I prefer cake and scones," Betty replied rather bluntly, "so what made you choose this village then?"

"I've wanted to move out to the country for a while now, slower pace of life and all that," Emma reddened under Betty's unflinching stare.

"And where have you come from?" Betty asked.

"York, I used to live in York," Emma said quickly, "anyway, so much still to do," she was clearly trying to end the conversation politely.

"Come on Betty, I'll see you home, then I have to rush back to get changed for Jazzercise this evening."

"I don't know why you put yourself through that each week, Flora. When I was your age we kept trim by scrubbing the front step and..." Betty's voice trailed off as she left, with Flora raising her eyebrows apologetically at Emma, waving quickly and then following in Betty's wake. The fresh air was a welcome relief after the small shop, and Flora was glad of the chance to breathe it in deeply and to put the uncomfortable encounter with Joe out of her mind.

NINETEEN

Flora sat in front of her vintage typewriter, freshly showered and in her pyjamas after her weekly bout of exercise. Her enthusiasm for writing was bubbling over once again following her chance encounter with Lizzie, the artist from earlier. The first story, a space adventure, sat neatly typed on sheets of white paper beside her, and Flora had just started the next story, an expedition to the North Pole, when her telephone rang.

"Hello?"

"Flora, it's Harry, just wanted to check we're still on for the sweet shop contract signing at the tearoom at eleven tomorrow morning? I may be a few minutes late as I have the reading of Ray's will first."

"Of course, I have it in my diary," Flora said, unwelcome images of the scene at the sweet shop earlier coming unbidden to her mind, "Poor Shona, I hope that all goes well for her. I suppose she can't win, really – if she inherits something, the police may well hold that against her, if she doesn't she and Aaron are left with nothing."

"Indeed," Harry agreed sombrely, "the only other thing is the rents. Per your instruction, I lowered them to match market rates and that came into force on the first of September. I've already had some thankful messages from local folk."

"Oh that's excellent, Harry, thank you. What would I do without you to keep on top of things? Please don't ever retire completely!"

Harry chuckled, "I don't have any intention of that, not in the near future anyway. Betty keeps me feeling young!"

Flora smiled at his implication and ended the call, happy that Harry had sounded so lively.

When her phone rang again a couple of minutes later, Flora answered immediately assuming it must be Harry having forgotten something.

"Flora, sorry to bother you," Flora stiffened when she heard Phil's voice on the end of the line.

"Hello, Phil," she replied cautiously.

"How are you, Flora?"

"I'm fine," Flora wished he would get straight to the point.

"I was just wondering, now that Ray is, ah, well dead, if you would reconsider allowing me to look at my information and his too, from Harold's files."

"I've given you my answer on that already, Phil, I haven't changed my mind."

"Please, Flora, what harm can it do now?"

"A lot of harm, what if there is other stuff in there? Delicate information that should stay buried? Besides, it's not my place to share private details about a deceased man. I've told you, the files are stored away. I don't have easy access to them... Phil?" Realising he had hung up on her, Flora tried to squash the rising sense of panic which threatened to engulf her. Calling Reggie over from his perch, she felt immediately comforted by his presence. Perhaps it was time to get Adam involved with this matter, after all?

The next day dawned with a chill in the air that heralded summer's time was nearly over for another year. Despite her aching limbs from Jazzercise, Flora woke up with a sense of purpose, aware that she had a lot to get done this day. She chose to forgo a sundress and opted for a smart navy trouser suit instead, chosen particularly for her appointment with Harry and Emma. There were times, Flora had decided, that it was appropriate to look the part of estate owner and 'lady of the manor.' It wasn't ideal, since she planned on going up to the farm shop if George's regular bakery drop off didn't materialise, but Flora brought her floral wellington boots with her in case the need arose to go up to the farm. These could easily replace her red kitten heels if need be.

Happy that she looked smart enough, with her hair in a neat low ponytail, Flora picked up the boots and her red leather handbag, and followed Reggie out of the front door and along the path to the tearoom. As she had suspected, there was no delivery from George, which Flora really didn't mind, as she hoped he was looking after Pepper instead. Popping a note on the door to say she would be open in half an hour, and leaving Reggie on his perch in the locked tearoom, Flora quickly walked up to the garage beside the manor house for her car. It had been a couple of weeks since she had needed to use it, and she hoped the engine would start without any bother.

Thankfully, for once the stars aligned and everything went smoothly. There was no sign of further attempted forced entry when Flora quickly checked the side door of the big house, the car started easily, and she drove to the Houghton's farm without incident. Breathing in the earthy farm aroma, which was a combination of the smell of animal dung and late summer warmth, Flora changed into her rubber boots and made her way across the farmyard and to the small shop which was in a barn just to the side of the main farmhouse.

Lily greeted Flora with a hug and a wide smile, thrilled to have Flora visit her little business for the first time. She pointed out all of the produce which they had grown themselves on the farm and then showed off her selection of cakes and treats. Flora felt immediately at ease, as she always did in Lily's company, and they were soon chatting away as Flora picked out the things she wanted for the tearoom.

"Such a shame about poor Pepper Jones. As if she hasn't been through enough already," Lily whispered, although they were the only two in the small shop area.

"It really is. Have you spoken to her?" Flora didn't want to let slip anything she and Tanya had been told in confidence the previous day, if Lily didn't already have the facts.

"I have, I popped into the village yesterday evening to get the local paper from Baker's Rise Essential Supplies, and as I was coming back I saw Pepper being dropped off outside their home in a police car of all things! Well, I went over to see what was up, and she looked like she'd spent the whole day crying, poor woman. Her face was red and blotchy, and she was shaking like a leaf."

"Yes, I saw her earlier in the day in the tearoom – she was already upset then, and it sounds like she was suffering all afternoon too, bless her."

"Well, I helped George get her into the house and settled on the sofa, and it all spilled out of her. They'd questioned her at the station and then let her go, but she's still worried she'll be called back in and arrested. Poor woman, I'm sure she wouldn't harm a fly. Then there's the awful truth about their Anna – she told me that too!"

"I was wondering, though, do you know who it was that could have been stalking Anna like that all those years ago?" Flora asked, "Would it definitely have been Ray? When they made their last move and sent her fleeing, it must've been bad enough to warrant the girl running away from everyone and everything she loved."

"I guess no one will know now, given that the two main suspects, in my opinion anyway, are both dead. Who knows if it was Harold or Ray? I really can't imagine it being anyone else though. To think, all these things happening and no one ever knows until after the event," Lily said, her normally cheery face for once full of concern.

"It's a bad business all round. I'll be glad when it's all over, but I can't stand the thought of them arresting Shona," Flora whispered, "I honestly don't believe she could've done it any more than Pepper."

"I agree, but who does that leave, I wonder? One of his exes? Someone else from the village? I've known these people all my life, and I can't abide the fact that I could be living alongside a neighbour who would do such a thing. It was bad enough when we learnt about Enid Wright and now this!" Lily's voice rose along with her emotions, and Flora empathised completely with her.

"Yes, the village certainly feels like it's under a black cloud right now," Flora said sadly, as Lily rang her purchases through the till and bagged them up.

"I haven't forgotten about your pie lessons," Lily said regretfully, as Flora was about to leave, "it's just now's not the best time…"

"Of course," Flora said, hugging the other woman before heading back out to her car. She waved at Stan who was just coming from the nearest field in his old green tractor, his trusty dog Bertie by his side on the seat.

Flora felt chilled through, and not just because of the change in the weather. So much suspicion and conflict, so much history and so many secrets. Flora began to realise that her idea of a quiet life in the country may just have been pie in the sky.

TWENTY

When Flora got back to the tearoom and carried her baked goods in, Reggie was sat on the coffee machine, looking as if butter wouldn't melt.

"What have you been up to? You mustn't sit on there, sometimes it gets hot!" Flora said worriedly, eying him suspiciously.

"Welcome to the tearoom!" Reggie squawked, clearly trying to butter her up. Flora smiled at him and glanced around, wondering what destruction he was trying both to hide and to make up for. Spotting the table in the far corner, closest to his perch, Flora let out a shriek of dismay. The lace doily looked to have been pulled from under the crockery which rested on top of it – or rather had done – now, two fancy cups and saucers lay smashed on the floor, half covered in the doily as if it were a shroud.

"Reginald Parrot!" Flora exclaimed as she dumped the cakes on the counter and rushed over to inspect the damage, "What is this? Who has done this?" she asked, gesticulating towards the floor, even though they both knew the answer.

"You sexy beast!" Reggie said, flying over and landing on Flora's shoulder, trying to worm himself back into her good graces.

"Don't be rude! Oh dear, best get this cleared up before Harry and Emma get here," Flora sighed, shrugging out of her suit jacket and replacing it with her favourite apron. Decorated in bold sunflowers, it normally never failed to make Flora feel more cheery. Today, though, Flora guessed it would take a lot to improve her mood.

"Perch, now," Flora said sternly, and Reggie flew silently across, bowing his head when he reached his stand. Flora felt slightly sorry for him, until she looked down again at the mess on the floor. *No*, she decided, *he will have to be remorseful for a bit longer this time!*

At five minutes to eleven, Emma arrived, looking a picture in a fitted pink midi dress and matching gloves.

"Morning Emma," Flora smiled, "you look lovely!

Another beautiful pair of gloves to match your outfit! You're like a modern Audrey Hepburn."

"Oh thank you, Flora," Emma blushed and turned to look around for Reggie.

"Well, it's a very good look on you," Flora said, handing Emma a menu, "Harry said he might just be a few minutes late as he has a prior meeting."

"Of course, there's no hurry. And why is our feathered friend so quiet today?" Emma asked, eying Reggie who sat huffing on his perch, his eyes alert, but his pose defensive.

"Oh, he's just in time out!" Flora laughed, "He's on the naughty perch for smashing some crockery. I don't think he intended to do it, I think the thought of playing with the doily was just too much temptation when I was out!"

"Oh, he's such a cutie," Emma smiled and waggled her finger in Reggie's direction, "cheeky birdie!"

"Good morning, ladies, apologies for my tardiness," Harry said, blustering through the door with a large, worn leather briefcase under his arm.

"How are we all today?" He asked politely, though Flora thought she detected a certain strain to Harry's usually relaxed features and wondered how the will reading had gone. It would be inappropriate to ask, though, especially with Emma here, and knowing Harry to be a stickler for confidentiality. Flora didn't want to put him in an uncomfortable position.

Instead, she simply replied, "Very well, thank you, Harry. Shall we get to the business of the contract first and then have tea and cake?"

"That sounds perfect," Emma replied as Harry nodded, and so the three of them sat at Emma's table while Harry removed the papers in question from his case.

"So, Miss Blenkinsopp, we have already discussed this verbally, there should be nothing to surprise you, but please do read through everything before signing and dating here, here, and here," Harry indicated the places which had each been marked with a small cross.

Flora watched as Emma read and then signed the documents, though was slightly distracted by the feeling of small projectiles hitting her neck. Turning slightly, she saw Reggie mischievously launching seeds at her from his food box attached to the perch. At any other time, Flora would have smiled, but right now, she had to bite her tongue to stop from shouting at him. *Silly bird!* Her first important action as owner of the estate and he couldn't even behave for five minutes!

When Flora looked back, Emma was adding her signature to the final page. She added the date in her pretty cursive script and Harry smiled widely, "Excellent, excellent, thank you. Now Flora, here, here and here please."

Flora signed where indicated, and then stood to make the drinks. Something niggled at the back of her mind, but she had neither the energy nor the inclination to think deeply on what it could be. If it were important, she knew it would come to her eventually. The morning, which should have been pleasant given the activities she had carried out so far, had felt strained and stressful. On top of the couple of weeks she'd had, Flora wanted nothing more than to hibernate back at the coach house for a while, with her typewriter and the silly bird who was now cuddling up to her neck as if nothing had happened.

"Thank you both so much, I'll have the money for the deposit and first month's rent transferred today," Emma gushed.

"Of course, thank you," Flora replied absentmindedly. Money was the least of her worries at the moment.

When Harry and Emma had left, and Flora had washed the dishes, she finally sat down and took her feet out of her smart shoes, wiggling her toes which were used to being in sandals. *Just a few minutes of peace,* Flora thought to herself, though the universe seemed to have other ideas. At that same moment, the tearoom door opened on a gust of wind and Will Monkhouse blew in, swiftly followed by Shona.

All thoughts of herself forgotten, Flora jumped up to welcome her friend, "Shona, how are you? I've been getting my daily reports from Betty but it's so lovely to see you in the flesh, so to speak! I've been so worried!" Flora gave the younger woman a huge hug and invited the pair to sit down with her, surreptitiously putting her shoes back on.

"Aw thank you Flora, I'm really grateful. It's been a hell of a time, I can't lie, and I think it's probably still not over. I'm just relieved that Aaron is back at school and has a more normal routine, and that we've been allowed to collect a few extra clothes and things from the pub," Shona's lip quivered and Will was quick to put his arm around her shoulders. Flora noticed that the young woman had lost even more weight and looked awfully pale.

"Let me make us some sweet tea and get you some of Lily's delicious carrot cake, that'll do wonders to give you some energy," Flora said quickly, jumping up to give the couple a moment of privacy for Shona to compose herself.

Drinks made, and Shona and Will both entertained and distracted by Reggie's clownish antics pretending the window ledge was a tightrope, Flora sat down with them and poured from the pretty floral teapot.

"So," Flora said quietly, "is it okay to ask how the will reading went?"

"It is. It went... well in one respect and badly in another."

"Oh?"

"Yes, it went well in that, despite that awful woman and her two loutish sons turning up and making demands, Harry says what is written in black and white and signed by my dad can't be disputed – Aaron and I get everything. I mean," Shona rushed on, "I know you own the pub building and land, Flora, as part of the estate and everything. I just meant that we get to take over the lease according to the terms, and we get what little my dad owned. I'm not bothered about how much, I just didn't want it going to... I would have had nowhere else to go and... well, you know," she stopped, her eyes brimming with tears.

"Of course," Flora rested her hand over Shona's, "of course the lease of the pub building goes to you, I wouldn't see it any other way. And I'm sure we can arrange to pause the rent till you get yourself back on your feet, I'll speak to Harry about it. So, what was bad about the reading?" Flora thought she could guess, but didn't want to assume.

"Well, I can imagine the police are going to hold this against me, aren't they? Me being the only beneficiary," Shona asked, looking beseechingly at Will, big fat tears running down her face.

"Don't worry, honey, it'll be okay," Will comforted her as best he could. In reality, although they all hoped it would turn out fine, no one could say for sure. Flora's stomach lurched at the thought of Shona being formally arrested. Was this the motive the police had been holding out for?

"Did you know what was in the will beforehand?" Flora asked, trying to find any glimmer of positivity.

"None at all. But how could I prove that?"

"I'm not sure. Maybe if we get Harry to swear that the

documents were locked away from the moment your dad signed them?" Flora suggested.

"I'm not sure that would prove that Ray hadn't told Shona that he'd left everything to her," Will replied morosely, raking his hands through his messy hair.

"I'm so sorry I can't be more helpful," Flora sighed as she took a sip of her tea, feeling the regret deep inside herself.

"Please don't apologise, I know no one can help me now," Shona sobbed loudly with that admission, and snuggled her face into Will's chest. It was such a sad scene, that Flora felt the lump form in her own throat and had to look away. Even Reggie was subdued, sitting on the window sill watching them all intently. Something needed to be done, but what?

TWENTY-ONE

Friday thankfully came and went without incident. There was no sign of Adam, but so too was Blackett absent from the village, and no one arrived to charge Shona. Flora was glad of the reprieve from stress and speculation. Then Saturday morning again was quite normal, with a few visitors to the tearoom but nothing more to note as far as the case was concerned. Flora began to wonder if this wasn't just the calm before the storm, and then got annoyed with herself for the negative attitude she'd developed lately. Even Reggie seemed to be picking up on her unsettled state, and spent more and more time on his perch. This in turn caused Flora to feel guilty and irritated with herself, and so the cycle perpetuated.

Early on Saturday afternoon, Pat Hughes called in to

the café to update Flora on the investigation into the tampered-with lock on the manor house – mainly to say that there was no update, though he did manage to get through two slices of banana loaf and a pot of English Breakfast tea in the imparting of this news! Basically, he explained, the powers that be had said it wasn't worth taking fingerprints since the building hadn't actually been broken into, plus there were a multitude of builders in and out leaving their prints leading up to that day, and new locks had now been fitted anyhow to hopefully prevent a reoccurrence. Flora had suspected that this would be the resolution, as unsatisfactory as it felt. She mentioned to Pat about her suspicions around Joe Stanton and he duly noted them in his little black notebook, whilst telling Flora that there wasn't enough evidence to go on for him to investigate. All in all, Pat recommended Flora put it from her mind and move on. He then took a third slice of banana bread with him for good measure, to eat whilst he made his rounds of the village. Flora couldn't complain, the man had done his job after all, but it only served to add to her disquiet.

Finally, at mid-afternoon on Saturday – when Flora was considering shutting up shop for the day and heading home to put her feet up and watch an old black and white Miss Marple film she had recorded –

things finally turned around, as the Marshall family all tumbled into the tearoom, one after the other. The three girls, Evie, Charlotte and little Megan were all windswept, with mud up their leggings and bright, rosy cheeks. Their parents, Reverend Marshall and his wife, Sally, followed, also wearing hiking boots and looking a very healthy colour. Flora smiled and welcomed them in, their bubbling energy exactly what she needed to drag her out of her gloomy rut.

"Girls! What a lovely surprise!" Flora exclaimed, nearly toppling backwards as three little pairs of arms charged forwards and grappled to hug her around the waist.

"Mrs. Miller! Mummy and Daddy said we can have hot chocolates… with marshmallows!" Evie practically squealed with the excitement she felt. Charlotte, who was the shyer of the three, stepped back, her cheeks blushing after briefly hugging Flora, while little Megan took hold of Flora's hand and swung her arm up and down.

"Girls, girls, let Mrs. Miller breathe a bit," Sally said, smiling ruefully and ruffling Charlotte's bright red, curly hair.

"Ah don't worry," Flora replied happily, "they are just the tonic I needed!"

The family sat down at the table next to Reggie's perch, as chosen by the girls. Reggie himself, who had been rather rudely awoken from an afternoon snooze, was also in surprisingly good humour, letting the girls take turns at stroking his feathers, and then jumping round the table, strutting as he lapped up all the attention. Thankfully, he also refrained from uttering any of his more colourful phrases, and instead chirped "Welcome!" each time one of the girls tickled his head.

"Thank you for this," James Marshall said, as Flora served up five huge hot chocolates, with lemon cake for the adults and marshmallows for the girls, "though I must admit it's not just your fine refreshments we have come for."

"Oh?" Flora was curious and pulled a chair over to the table when Sally offered she sit with the family.

"Yes," Evie piped up, "I told Mummy and Daddy all about Reggie's adventures – you know, the ones you told us about in church last week – and we all wanted to hear more!"

"She actually hasn't talked about much else all week," Sally laughed, "even starting a new school in the village has paled in comparison!"

"Well, then I mustn't disappoint," Flora chuckled, "let

me think, did I tell you the one about Reggie learning to surf in Australia and meeting a shark?" Flora made it up on the spot.

"No!" the girls squealed in unison.

"Well, then let's start with that story," Flora found she was in her element, imagining Reggie's hilarious antics, which made the children guffaw with laughter. Even the vicar and his wife were laughing along, and Reggie cocked his head and puffed out his feathers proudly, as if he knew the tale was about him.

"It's a shame I don't have a cosy corner, with beanbags or such," Flora mused out loud, when she had finished a third story, "though I don't think there's enough space in here, there are other stable buildings attached behind this one though, ready to be renovated..." An idea formed in Flora's head which she was desperate to note down, but waited politely as her guests got up to leave.

"Yes, it's such a shame there's no longer a village library," James added thoughtfully, "I asked around and was told the small one they had was closed in the nineties."

"That is a shame," Flora answered distractedly, feeling a flicker of excitement in her stomach as her small idea sparked to life.

As soon as she had waved goodbye to the lovely family, Flora sat straight back down at the messy table – cluttered as it was with dirty cups and plates – and took her silk-covered notebook from the pocket of her apron. In it, she began to note down the bare bones of an idea to transform the next part of the old stable block into a book shop which incorporated a library corner.

Goodness me, Flora thought, scribbling furiously and getting rather carried away, *we could even have a gift section!* She knew, of course, that she should be focusing both her attention and her finances on the big house, but that would take many months, years perhaps, before it could be opened as a country house hotel. A bookshop, however, could be up and running in a few months if Flora could get the builders back to convert the second stable block and help her refurbish the place. It felt so lovely to have something new to think about, that Flora let herself be immersed in ideas of book shelves in the shape of trains and dragons, of beautiful candles and scarves to sell, and of a cosy book nook where she could both tell and sell her stories of Reggie the Intrepid Parrot.

It was past closing time when Flora finished clearing

up and mopping the mud from the floor. She didn't mind, though – far from it – the afternoon had been good for her soul and given her much to ponder on!

TWENTY-TWO

Another lovely surprise awaited Flora when she arrived back at the coach house with Reggie. Carrying some cake and the rest of the banana loaf, as the shop would be closed on Sunday, Flora was delighted to see Bramble's car pulled up outside.

"Adam!" she exclaimed, "this is a lovely surprise!"

"Hello, love, sorry to turn up unannounced, I thought you'd be home earlier. I've just arrived, mind, so not to worry!"

"Of course, you can come round anytime. I stayed a little later to jot down some ideas, I've had such a lovely afternoon. Have you met the new vicar and his family?" Flora couldn't stop speaking, she was so happy.

Reggie swooped in as soon as Flora had opened the door and the pair followed him into the house. Flora deposited the cakes on the kitchen counter, and turned to find Adam looking at her intently, "What is it?" she wondered aloud.

"Oh, just you, your eyes are sparkling and your cheeks brighter than I've seen for a while now. It's lovely to see you happy again... you're quite beautiful, you know," Adam himself blushed when he said it, and Flora walked two steps across the small kitchen and put her arms around his waist, leaning back to look into his eyes.

"You're not half bad yourself, you know," she whispered, watching as his head angled down to kiss her.

It was such a sweet, tender embrace, and Flora let out a small sigh when Adam finally pulled away.

"How long do you have?" she asked him, aware that he was normally en route to work appointments.

"All evening, I'm off duty, off call, and don't intend to even mention work once!"

"That's perfect, then," Flora said, her good mood

ricocheting even further up the happy scale, "we could eat and watch a movie? I was going to watch a detective film, but I think that might be a bit too much like work for you!"

"Yes," Adam grinned, "a bit like a busman's holiday! Let's find something more lighthearted, shall we?"

"Perfect," Flora grabbed a bottle of wine from the fridge and saw that Adam carried a plastic bag with his favourite beer in it. Getting two glasses from the cupboard, they settled in for a cosy evening, and Flora felt the remaining tension drain from her body. With Reggie settled on her knee, and Adam's arm around her shoulders as they sat on the sofa, Flora's mind couldn't have been further from the sad events of recent weeks.

"Things will get better once the case is over. Lots more evenings like this," Adam promised as Flora walked him to the door later that night. It was past eleven and she couldn't help yawning. Even Reggie hadn't bothered making sure he escorted their visitor out, preferring to stay on the wool blanket on the couch. It was the first time Adam had mentioned the case, having kept his word and not said anything about work the whole time he was there. To be honest, Flora had managed to push it from her mind, and she now reluctantly let herself be reminded that a good friend was still suspected of murder and a culprit still on the loose – Adam only had to say the word 'case' and the whole course of events flashed through Flora's mind once again.

She was therefore distracted when they reached the front entrance, and it was Adam who reached down to the welcome mat in front of the door and said, "Who would be sending you mail at this time of night?"

"What's that?" Flora, trying to peer over Adam's shoulder, had no idea what he was referring to.

"A white envelope, your name but no address, posted through the letterbox. I'll open it love, something doesn't feel quite right to me, could you get me a knife from the kitchen? And a sandwich bag?"

"Of course."

As Adam followed her back through to the kitchen, Flora felt a ball of anxiety begin to knot in her chest. She watched closely as Adam slid the knife under the edge of the envelope and deftly slit the top open. He used the sandwich bag as an impromptu glove over his hand and pulled the single sheet of paper free. Unfolding it slowly over the sink, in case it contained some harmful substance, both Adam and Flora let out a sigh of relief to see that it simply contained a message made up of words cut out from a magazine – startlingly reminiscent of the letters Harold had used to blackmail the villagers, in fact, though those were made up of old newspaper clippings.

"Well, what do we have here?" Adam studied the sheet, and Flora found herself once again peering over him to get a closer look. Even squinting her eyes, Flora struggled to focus on the three short sentences, inwardly promising herself that she would sort out some reading glasses when she went to Alnwick on Monday. She would have liked to blame the dim light, or the angle she was reading from, but Flora knew the truth – it was middle age setting in.

"No one wants you here. You've caused enough trouble. Leave or pay the price," Flora read aloud, "Well, I mean, goodness, that's not…" before she realised it, Flora's breaths were coming in short, sharp gasps and her eyes were filled with tears.

"Hey, love, it's okay, take a few deep breaths. Here, with me, in… and out… in… and out… well done, I've got you," still holding the letter in his 'gloved' hand, Adam brought his other arm around Flora's shoulders and pulled her close, kissing the top of her hair as she struggled to bring her breathing back under control, "There you go, you're okay."

His voice was soothing and reassuring, and Flora turned her head into Adam's side, embarrassed that he should see her in such a state, "It just came as such a shock," she whispered, when she thought she could trust her voice to work.

"Of course it did. Don't you think any more on it, I'll have it dusted for prints tomorrow and we'll treat it as the serious threat it is. What about for now – will you be okay? I have work first thing, but I can stay the night if you like? – on the sofa bed – if it'll make you feel safer?"

"That's so sweet, thank you, but I'll be fine. Really," Flora wasn't sure if she was trying to convince him or herself, "I've got Reggie to protect me," she gave a watery smile, and Adam took his arm back so that he could manoeuvre the letter into the bag without touching it.

"Okay, but you call me at the slightest hint of anything. I'm going to get the station to contact Pat Hughes first thing in the morning and fill him in too."

"Do you think it's related to the door thing, at the big house?"

"If you mean, do I think it's Joe Stanton, then yes, I think he's the most likely suspect for both. Whether we can prove it, now that's a different matter entirely – unless he confesses of course. If there's even one fingerprint of his anywhere on there, he'll certainly have to come in to answer a few questions," Adam attempted a smile that verged on a grimace, and put the evidence in his inside jacket pocket for safekeeping.

"Shall I just go to church and everything as normal, then?" Flora asked, hating the quiver in her voice.

"Yes, act as if you haven't received it. Show no nerves, if you can, okay?" He pulled Flora in for one last hug and then all too soon Adam was gone and Flora was left alone. Resting her back against the wooden door, whose locks she had just checked twice to make doubly sure she was safe, Flora gave in to the sobs that wracked her body. Sinking down to sit on the very mat where the letter had sat not twenty minutes ago, Flora heard the flutter of wings as Reggie swooped in to land on her bowed head. Moving him onto her shoulder, Flora drew comfort from the feel of his feathers and his little beating heart against her, as she let the tears fall.

TWENTY-THREE

It was a rather subdued Flora who made her way
through the village and up the path to church the next
morning. She had barely slept, having sat awake for
ages and then succumbing to fitful dreams. As a result,
even her emergency routine of a small bit of concealer
and foundation, some blusher and a brush of mascara,
couldn't hide her saggy, pale cheeks and bloodshot
eyes. Flora chose a sombre outfit in dark brown, to
match her mood, and accessorized it with an even
darker black scarf. As per the Sunday tradition in the
village, she shoved a small black hat on her head,
complete with front netting, though Flora kept that
pushed back. It was one of the few hats she owned,

and had previously only been worn for funerals. Flora knew that it would stand out amongst the other women, who would no doubt still be in late summer colours, but on this occasion she really didn't care. She had already received a phone call and two texts from Adam checking she was okay and apologising for having to be at work. Flora understood – besides, she didn't want to be the woman who needed mollycoddling – and hoped she had reassured him, though no doubt he could see straight through the false cheer in her voice.

If the vicar noticed the change in Flora from the previous afternoon, he was polite enough not to let it show, and Flora was welcomed with his usual cheerfulness and gusto.

"Miss Flora! Miss Flora!" Evie ran up the aisle to welcome her, looking pretty in a beige dress that was covered in small squirrels.

"Good morning, Evie," Flora forced a smile, though knew she couldn't manage any stories this day.

"Please, Miss Flora, a story before the service starts?"

"I'm sorry, honey, I have a very sore throat today," Flora fibbed, "definitely next time though," she added, feeling awful when she saw the girl's downcast eyes and quivering lip and knew she had put them there.

"Let's leave Mrs. Miller to get settled, shall we?" Sally came to the rescue, smiling apologetically at Flora. Her astute eyes took in Flora's strained features, and Flora could tell that the kind woman knew something was amiss, though she thankfully asked no questions and simply led the girl away to where her sisters were sitting on the front pew.

Betty, on the other hand, was another story entirely. Flora's behind had barely touched the hard wood of the pew when the older woman has grasped hold of Flora's elbow, leant in close, and whispered, "has someone else died?"

"What? No!" Flora was shocked by the assumption. She knew she looked bad, but really?

"What is it then, lass?"

"I'll tell you after," Flora hissed back, even though she knew Betty was just being caring. Well, caring mixed with insatiable curiosity!

"What's this?" Harry asked from the other side of Betty.

"It's Flora, she looks like she's seen a ghost!" Betty answered, her voice a stage whisper that Flora was sure everyone in the small congregation had heard. Chancing a look behind her, Flora's eyes unfortunately locked first with Joe Stanton's, sitting two rows behind them. Being sure not to change her expression in anyway, though also not wanting to enter into a staring competition with the man, Flora's eyes skimmed across to the person sitting next to him – Emma Blenkinsopp.

"That's the first time I've seen Joe in church," Flora whispered to Betty as she turned back to face the front, where the vicar still hadn't appeared at the ornate lectern.

"Aye well, word has it his wife's gone and left him – back to live with her mother in Newcastle. He's been spending a lot of time in that new sweetie shop, if you know what I mean," Betty raised her wrinkled eyebrows suggestively and Flora's own eyes widened. She had certainly sensed a certain tension in the air when she had called in on Emma in the shop the other day, but it hadn't crossed her mind that Joe was married. Flora knew he was, of course, having seen him in the pub with his wife a few times in the past months, but it must have skipped her memory. Now Flora came to think of it, she hadn't seen them together recently. Not since that business with Harold's death and then Joe losing his job as postman. The ball of anxiety in Flora's stomach, there since last night, grew exponentially until she felt like she was about to be sick. It was as if dozens of sets of eyes were boring into her back, and she no longer knew which was friend and which foe. Not wanting to cause a scene, Flora made an excuse to Betty about needing to check something at the tearoom and rushed out of the side door nearest her.

"Flora!" Shona said, startled, as Flora nearly bumped into her on her way out of the church.

"I'm so sorry Shona," Flora could barely form a sentence, the panic having descended over her like a wave.

"Don't worry, we shouldn't be coming in this door," Shona indicated herself, Aaron and Will who stood just behind them, "we were trying to sneak in quietly! But you look a bit off colour, Flora, if you don't mind me saying. Come and have a sit down."

She led Flora to one of the small wooden benches which were positioned on the grass under the trees, lining the path around the church. They heard the organ chords of the first hymn, as Flora struggled to catch her breath. Will had thoughtfully taken Aaron off to play on the Green for a few minutes, giving the women some privacy.

"There you are lass!" Betty came rushing around the corner from the front entrance of the church, her blue felt hat askew, "I had to wait till the song started to get out unnoticed. Now what's this all about?" She sat down on the other side, so that Flora was now flanked by both women, with Shona's arm around her shoulders and Betty clasping her hands.

"Has something else happened... with the case?" Betty whispered, casting a worried glance at Shona.

"Do you know they're coming to arrest me and that's why you're so upset?" tears started falling down Shona's sweet face, and the sight of them caused the dam to break for Flora too, with heavy wet droplets soon streaming over her cheeks and down onto her scarf.

"No, no, nothing like that," Flora was quick to reply, devastated that she'd unduly caused Shona extra distress, "I just had some... bad news last night. Nothing to do with the case, I promise. I'm fine, Adam was with me, it just knocked me off kilter. I shouldn't have come out this morning, is all."

"Well, you're going to be just fine with us," Betty tapped Flora's hand to reinforce her point, "if you don't want to talk about it that's okay, but we're not going to leave you to be upset alone. Come on, we'll all go back to mine for a pot of tea and a slice of cake. Shona here, and young Aaron were helping me bake yesterday afternoon, so we've got quite the selection..," her voice trailed off as Flora tuned out and allowed herself to be led from the bench and down the path towards the Green. She really wasn't feeling sociable, but there was no way to get out of it now, not without upsetting and worrying both women even more. Flora had the feeling it was going to be a long day.

TWENTY-FOUR

It was a completely different Flora who woke up the next morning. Having managed to extricate herself from Betty's maternal attentions at four the previous afternoon, Flora had rushed home to a very disgruntled parrot, who was annoyed at having been left alone so long. After giving Reggie a veritable fruit salad to snack on – blueberries, raspberries, grapes, orange and apple slices – Flora had sat down at her typewriter, threaded a new sheet of paper onto the roller, and began typing out everything that was on her mind. It was an exercise which she had repeated many times during her marriage to Gregory – particularly near the end – and had served her well, though of course then she didn't have the added bonus of a beautiful vintage typewriter to work on.

*If I can get through that marriage and then the divorce, come
to a completely new and rather strange place and start
afresh, all by myself, I can cope with this!* Flora told herself
as she let her thoughts flow through her fingers and
form a string of black words on the white page. She
didn't care whether they made sense, it just mattered
that she got them out of her head. That done, Flora had
soaked in a bubble bath, spent time trying to teach
Reggie some new phrases, spoken on the phone to
Adam, read some of her latest romance novel and then
had the best night of sleep she'd had in a while. She
had deliberately avoided checking the 'welcome' mat
for more unwelcome messages, but had been sorely
tempted on more than one occasion. Instead, Flora
distracted herself with the radio and with dancing with
Reggie as she dressed that Monday morning.

As a result, Flora was more than ready to face the new
week, and, taking a final look at herself in the
bathroom mirror before she headed out, was pleased to
see that some of the colour had returned to her cheeks
and the sparkle to her eyes. Tanya, being the
sweetheart she was, had agreed to open the tearoom
and stay all morning, giving Flora the chance to drive
to Alnwick with Reggie for his preliminary portrait
appointment. After that, Flora was hoping to have her
eyes tested and to, finally, acquire some reading

glasses! She might even push the boat out and have a haircut while she was in the larger town.

It was certainly a case of choosing to be happy and positive, as Flora knew that deep down her anxiety about the threatening letter still bubbled below the surface, just waiting to erupt if she let it. It was a beautiful early autumn day, which held the promise of warmth and sunshine later in the afternoon, so Flora wore a delicately-embroidered cream blouse and a green cotton skirt which swished pleasantly around her shins. In shoes of the same green, and with a thin cream jacket to ward off the morning chill, Flora made her first attempt at putting Reggie into the portable cage for travelling which she had bought online and had delivered that weekend. It was more of a case really, with a stiff cotton outer layer, transparent plastic windows, breathing vents and three small perches inside.

"Where to now? Where to now?" Reggie squawked, refusing to walk from Flora's hand into the new cage.

"Just for a trip in the car," Flora cajoled, wondering if he even understood what 'car' meant. She understood his trepidation, but they really did need to get going if they were hoping to make the thirty minute car journey and arrive at Reggie's appointment on time.

In the end, Flora used a juicy green grape as temptation, and put her whole outstretched hand into the case, with Reggie trying to run back up to her wrist as she gradually tipped him in. It was not ideal, and Flora felt slightly guilty for persevering, but she couldn't have the bird flapping around the car uncontained – it wouldn't be safe for either of them.

They finally set off and once she was out of the village, and could see it disappearing in her rear-view mirror, Flora had to admit to feeling relief – as if a weight had been lifted from her shoulders – and she began to enjoy the drive through the Northumberland countryside. Flora had never driven north of Baker's Rise, always heading south to Morpeth. Alnwick was an even bigger market town than Morpeth, with its own huge castle and famous gardens, as well as the being home to the biggest used book store in Europe, housed in an old train station. Flora knew she wouldn't have time to visit those places today, but she planned to drive past and have a quick look on her way there. The leaves were just beginning to change colour on some of the many trees which lined the narrow roads, and Flora felt the pleasure that came from knowing her two favourite seasons were beginning. She loved the cosiness of autumn and winter, and was looking forward to hopefully seeing some snow this year, though she had been told it could get quite bad this far north if it fell heavily. To be honest, that excited Flora even more – the thought of being snowed in, with the fire roaring and Reggie beside her, ooh Adam as well even… Flora's thoughts trailed off to happy places and before long she had arrived at the address which Lizzie had given her, and which Flora was grateful she had Satnav to find!

Hidden down a country lane, about half a mile outside the main town, Flora pulled up on the driveway next to Lizzie's studio. Attached to a large, white detached house, the studio was a single storey building, with an arrangement of hand-painted wooden signs outside. A small slice of polished wood caught Flora's eye, as she had a quick look at the display with Reggie's cage balancing in her arms. It looked to say The Rise, but Flora couldn't be sure that it wasn't The Rose as the script used for the white painted writing was very cursive and she was having to squint to try to make it out. In any case, she had Reggie's carrier to contend with and the little chap himself was making some none-too-happy noises from inside, so Flora hurried through the little door and into a huge studio. The roof was mostly comprised of one pointed glass skylight, almost like a pyramid on top of the room, which allowed light to flood the area, and highlighted the many pictures and portraits which were both hung on the walls and resting against them.

"Flora, I'm so glad you were able to find us, tucked away down this lane!" Lizzie emerged from behind a small desk, "and here's the star of the show, Reggie himself," she exclaimed, as Flora could no longer ignore the parrot's increasingly shrill squawks, and so let him out to hop onto the table.

"Bad bird! Bad bird!" Reggie aimed his displeasure at Flora, clearly feeling he needed to protest his recent incarceration, before puffing out his chest feathers and hopping onto Lizzie's offered hand.

"He's such a character," Lizzie laughed.

"Isn't he just," Flora replied, somewhat more sardonically, "I was just admiring your lovely house signs out front."

"Ah yes, my partner paints those actually, we get quite a good business in them from locals and from passing trade. Those are just examples really, you can have any name written up."

Flora thanked Lizzie and said she would think about it, while the other woman fussed over Reggie, and then placed him on a table, which had clearly been set out for the purpose, covered in a black tablecloth. Against the stark monotone background, the bird's beautiful green feathers stood out even more, and Lizzie admired his good looks.

"You'll make a gorgeous cover star of your own books, won't you?" Lizzie tickled Reggie's yellow head feathers affectionately.

Clearly lapping up the attention, Reggie strutted, preened and waddled his way from one corner of the table to the other, as Lizzie manoeuvered her easel into position.

"I'll just do some quick sketches today, and maybe a few photos to work from, if that's okay? Flora?"

Lizzie repeated herself to get Flora's attention. Flora herself was deep in thought and had completely tuned out of what was going on in the studio. The cursive handwriting had sent her back in her memory to the other day, when she had watched a certain young lady sign the contract for the sweet shop on Front Street. Flora had just assumed the signed initial was an 'E' but now she thought on it, it had looked more like an 'A'. And was she using her right or her left hand in those delicate gloves? Flora ran the picture through her mind and had the answer. Definitely her left. A cold chill ran up Flora's spine as she started to put two and two together.

Stop jumping to conclusions, she told herself quickly, trying to tamp down her rising panic.

"Flora, shall we get started?" Lizzie asked, rousing Flora from her own internal dialogue.

"Yes, thanks, sorry, I was in my own little world there! What a great setup you have here…" Flora moved onto autopilot, as she had in her previous life in business, making small talk whilst also creating her own internal observations. One thing Flora knew for sure – she wouldn't rush in with all guns blazing. She certainly didn't want to risk being a target like last time, so today she would take time to think things through, before contacting Adam with her suspicions.

TWENTY-FIVE

The drive which had seemed so relaxing and scenic on the way to Alnwick, felt never-ending and frustrating on the journey back to Baker's Rise. Having ditched the idea of a leisurely look around the small town after their appointment, plus any thoughts of eye tests and hairdressers, Flora instead wanted to get home and relieve Tanya in the tearoom as quickly as possible. She needed a moment of peace to go through her whole memory of the contract signing in her mind once again. Then, and only then, when she was sure there might be something to it and not just the fanciful imaginings of a brain desperate to clear Shona, would she contact Adam.

Flora's curiosity got the better of her, however, when

she drove down Front Street from the main road, and instead of turning left up to The Rise, she instead continued along the row of shops – *just to see if there's anyone in the sweet shop,* she told herself. Keeping the car crawling along the road at a snail's pace, intending to just look through the window of the shop from the comfort of her car, Flora caught sight of Betty hurrying along the street. The older woman looked to be on a mission, with her back hunched, her head down and her handbag swinging wildly on her arm, little Tina being dragged along behind. To Flora's dismay, she turned directly into the candy shop, whose door was standing open.

Pulling the car up onto the pavement, and grabbing Reggie's carry case as if on autopilot, Flora jumped out and ran the short distance back up the street to the shop in question. Before she'd even entered the small building, Flora could hear raised voices, and as she rushed into the main shop area – half fitted out with pink shelves and a large, white counter – she caught the end of the conversation in the back room. Flora couldn't see either of the women, but knew them to be Emma and Betty.

"That means nothing!" Emma shouted, "there are plenty of Blenkinsopp's, I'm sure!"

"Aye, but it came back to me, as I was watching 'Homes Under the Hammer,' that the name belonged to Ray's wife Patricia – it was her maiden name, I'm sure of it! – She loved those house programmes, didn't she Amelia?" Betty's indignant voice rose in pitch. Flora opened the door to the back room, just in time to see Emma give Betty a hard push in her abdomen, before fleeing up the stairs which led to the flat above. Betty herself seemed to ricochet off the small kitchen counter top, before crumpling back onto the floor, her face ashen. With Betty dropping little Tina's lead in the process, the dog raced up the stairs, barking after Emma, and Flora had the quick thinking to unlatch Reggie's cage and let him follow her up. Perhaps the two animals could pester the younger woman long enough to keep her busy while Flora tended to Betty.

"It's Amelia, Patricia's daughter," Betty whispered, though her voice faltered from pain.

"I know, I had just guessed as much before I got here," Flora replied, whilst simultaneously dialling 999 for an ambulance, "oh Betty, I wish you hadn't confronted her alone, tell me where it hurts."

"My side and my hip, leave me and go after her," Betty looked as if she was about to pass out, as Flora gave the address details and asked the emergency operator to also send the police. She left the phone with Betty and turned her attention reluctantly to the younger woman.

Shrieks could be heard from the upstairs room and, after making Betty as comfortable as possible with her handbag for a pillow, Flora ventured cautiously up the narrow staircase. Emma, or Amelia as she really was, was there, lifting a small suitcase onto the single bed. The room was empty apart from that and a tall, modern wardrobe, and Flora was met with the sight of the younger woman fighting against the small terrier who had hold of her trouser leg and was growling whilst tugging furiously, and the green bird who flapped around her head. Flora couldn't tell if Reggie was actually angry, or simply trying to get attention from the young lady he so admired. Either way, the little team of two were doing a good job of keeping the woman in question distracted. Aware that there was no way to escape for Amelia, but by the narrow staircase she herself had just climbed, Flora turned silently to go back the way she had come.

"Not so fast!" The snarled command was in sharp contrast to the pleasant young woman she had known thus far. Flora turned around to face her, maintaining as much distance as she could and aware that the open door to the staircase was at her back.

"Look Amelia, it is Amelia isn't it?" Flora asked softly.

"I prefer Emma now."

"Okay, Emma, I understand that you recently lost your mother. That must have been very painful, I'm sorry. You have badly hurt Betty, and I need to get back to her, but as it stands that's all you've done, so you're not in that much trouble, you just need to take a moment to calm down – unless there's something else you'd like to tell me?"

Emma flapped her hands at Reggie, who was still circling, and tried to kick her leg to remove Tina, both actions proving ineffectual. Her eyes were glazed over and she had the look of someone caught up in her own thoughts, "She loved him, you know, my mother. She always told me about the beautiful, idyllic village where they'd shared their lives – until he cheated on her, of course! But she forgave him, so blind was her love, and told me that when she died I was to find him here because she knew he'd welcome me back. She knew she was dying you see, inoperable brain tumour. So, I did as she wished, but when I confronted him in the pub that day, he told me he had so many children, always coming out of the woodwork, and we were two a penny to him! Of course, he had enough space in his heart for his golden girl, Shona," Emma hissed bitterly,

"I couldn't have been happier than I was when I heard she was the main suspect for killing him! Stupid bird!" Emma swiped a sideways blow at Reggie in her anger and sent him flying towards Flora, where he landed with a thump on the carpet.

"Reggie!" Flora shrieked, bending and taking a step forward to scoop the bird up in her arms. Doubled over as she was, Flora didn't see the attack coming, until she felt herself thrown back by a hefty kick to her shoulder. Already off balance, and using her arms to cradle Reggie, Flora couldn't stop her backwards momentum. In that split second, she resigned herself to flying down the stairs, until she felt something large and squishy breaking her fall.

"Careful, Flora! I've got you, lass!"

Never had Flora been so happy to hear the throaty tone of Pat Hughes' voice, as he caught her by both elbows, and she ended up with her back flattened against his ample stomach. Sirens could be heard in the distance, and Flora clutched Reggie to her chest, somewhat dazed. She could feel him breathing and his little chest rose and fell, but his eyes were closed.

A tidal wave of anger rose up in Flora in that instant and she shouted at Emma, "You stupid girl! How dare you!" She had the overriding desire to charge forwards and give Emma a taste of her own medicine, but Pat was already turning her towards the staircase.

"You go on and see to Betty. She filled me in, but she's drifting in and out of consciousness," Pat said, letting go of Flora's arms gently.

"She… she…"

"I know, let me deal with it, eh? I'll radio in and get those detectives back here," Pat eyed Emma, who had now slumped down onto the bed. Tina had finally let go of her, and the little dog shot down the stairs past Flora, keen to get to Betty.

"Okay, are you sure?" Flora didn't really want to leave anyone alone with the unstable woman.

Pat simply raised his eyebrows as if she was saying something silly, given his size and the fact he had police training, so Flora accepted his offer to get out of there. She made her way gingerly back down the stairs, her shoulder throbbing and her worry for Reggie almost choking her.

Two paramedics were just coming into the tiny back room, and the small space was quite full, so Flora hovered on the bottom stair, unsure where she should stand. She whispered reassurances to Reggie, whose eyes fluttered open at the sound of her voice, promising to get him to Will as soon as possible.

"We've got this in hand," one of the ambulance respondents told Flora, moving sideways so that she could squeeze past.

"Betty, will she be…?"

"Yes, they'll get her properly diagnosed and sorted up at the hospital, you look like you could do with some fresh air yourself."

"Yes, thank you," Flora whispered, aware of her head spinning, and the desire to get out into the clean air suddenly all she could think about.

TWENTY-SIX

"Flora, Flora love it's me," Flora came round to find herself sitting on the pavement outside the shop, her head bent between her knees, and Adam crouched down beside her. She winced and pulled away as he gently touched her bad shoulder.

"What's this? Are you hurt?" he couldn't disguise the worry in his voice.

"Kicked... in the shoulder. Where's Reggie?" Panic suddenly filled Flora as she realised she was no longer holding her sweet bird.

"Don't worry, see over there? Will and Shona are here and Will's taking a look at him, while Shona has Betty's little dog," Adam helped Flora to her feet, and held her against him whilst her head spun, "we'll need to get you checked out - you do have a habit of getting yourself into these pickles, don't you," Adam said gently, as they watched Blackett and Pat lead Emma from the building. Bemused, Flora noted that the young woman still wore her cotton gloves, though they struck Flora as silly now and no longer a well thought-out accessory – they had been a clever addition, certainly, whether deliberately or not. Those gloves had been the reason Emma had left no fingerprints on either the pie dish or the back door of the pub. Flora guessed she must have grabbed a pie from the pile Ray was carrying and struck her estranged father on the head with his own frozen dish in a flush of passion and anger, causing him to fall backwards down the stairs onto solid concrete. The image of Ray's body came back to haunt Flora's inner vision, and she quickly pulled away from Adam to be sick in the gutter.

"Aw love," Adam held her hair back and Flora leaned into him, "Well, I can see now why I thought it was Shona that I saw arguing with her father that day – she and Emma are both so similar from behind, with their shiny, long brown hair, and being the same stature and all."

"Where's Betty?" Flora's mind was working in fits and starts, as she wiped her mouth on her sleeve roughly, "she got here before me, we both must have put two and two together at the same time, but coming from different angles. I was more focused on the writing you see, and the fact Emma had signed 'A' instead of 'E' on the contract for the shop. I'm guessing that was a mistake, done out of habit, she perhaps didn't even realise herself that she'd done it..." Flora trailed off as she realised she was rambling. There would be time enough later to tell Adam the full story. No doubt she would be required to give a formal statement at some point in the near future.

"The ambulance crew took Betty away while Blackett was still upstairs with Pat and Emma. They wanted to get her out first on the stretcher. She was awake and seemed more concerned about you having just fainted, I think."

"Oh, bless her, I'll have to get to the hospital. I've left my bag and my car keys inside in the back room, I think," Flora started to pull away as if to go and find them.

"No, love, you're not driving anywhere else today, and that in there is now a crime scene. I'll fetch your things and take you to the hospital to see Betty as soon as I'm finished at the station, though that might be late. Perhaps Will and Shona would drive you? You definitely need to get that shoulder checked out. I think

that old bloke, Harry, went in the ambulance with
Betty."

"Thank goodness, I can't bear the thought of her being
by herself. That's fine then. I'll go and see to Reggie.
Thank you, Adam, I know you're working."

"Any time, love, I'll nip in now and grab your bag and
keys for you then I'll call you later, okay," he gave
Flora a quick, discreet peck on the cheek, and she could
see in Adam's eyes that he felt torn and didn't want to
leave her in her current state. Needs must, however,
and Flora gave his hand a small squeeze before
walking over to join Will and Shona.

Reggie nestled in the crook of Shona's bent arm, as
Will listened to his tiny, feathered chest with a
stethoscope.

"I've given him the once over," Will said, smiling at
Flora, "and I can't find any breaks in his wing bones.
He was lucky, just stunned I think. He'll be fine in an
hour or two."

"Thank goodness! Aw, Reggie, my sweet bird," Flora
took Reggie gently from Shona and cuddled him into
her.

His eyes popped open and, in true Reggie fashion, he

squawked softly, "She's a corker!" Flora had never been happier to hear one of his signature phrases!

Betty lay in the large hospital bed, looking tiny and frail in the thin nightgown the hospital must have provided. Flora was shocked to learn that the fall had broken Betty's left hip and so she was to stay in hospital with intravenous pain relief until she could have the operation to replace the hip joint in the next day or so. The kind ward nurse had allowed them to break the protocol of only two visitors per patient, so Flora, Harry, Will and Shona were all crowded into the small cubicle, having dropped Reggie at home to sleep off the shock of his injury.

"Betty, my love, it hurts my heart to see you in this state," Harry whispered as he sat to the side of the bed, holding Betty's hand. Betty herself simply nodded and smiled, no doubt somewhat dazed from the day's events and the medication she had been given, "I'll go to your cottage and bring you everything you need, you can help me write a list later." Harry himself looked pale and shaken, no doubt suffering from the same shock as the rest of the small group.

"I can't believe what you did for me – both of you," Shona said from Betty's other side, clutching the older woman's hand and looking from her to Flora. The relief was evident in her face as she spoke.

"I would do it again in a heartbeat," Flora said, though inside she wished that she had been able to stick to her original plan of informing the police of her suspicions. In no scenario, would she want to relive what had happened to Betty. She kept thinking that if only she had been paying more attention when Emma signed the contract, or if she had thought about the resemblance between Shona and Emma. As it was, there was no use focusing on 'what ifs' and Flora tried to shut them out of her mind to focus on Betty.

"That should be you cleared of any suspicion, now," Harry said to Shona, "and I'm sure they'll let you and Aaron move back into the pub soon. I will move into the cottage with Betty myself, to look after her while she recuperates. On that note, Betty," Harry paused and looked his beloved straight in the eyes. Flora got the impression it was as if there was only the two of them in the small space, given the looks they shared.

"We can go and give you two a moment of priv…" Flora began, only to be interrupted by Harry.

"No dear, wait a moment will you all? I'd like you all here for this. I'm too old to be getting down on one knee – I'd never get back up again! – but I want you to know, Betty dearest, that I would if I could."

"What are you saying?" Betty asked, her eyes suddenly alive with affectionate interest.

"Betty Lafferty, I love you with all my heart, and I'm not embarrassed to say so in front of all these young'uns! Would you do me the greatest honour and agree to become my wife, so I can love and cherish you for the rest of our days?"

Flora felt her eyes brim with tears, and noticed that Shona and Will were similarly affected.

"Of course I will," Betty whispered, angling her face to the side so that Harry could give her a sweet kiss on the lips.

"You've made me the happiest man," Harry said, stroking his hand down Betty's cheek, "Can we do it straight after the operation? In this hospital if needs be, as long as it's as soon as possible, I don't want to lose any more time to be together."

The tears were streaming down Betty's cheeks now, too, as she heartily agreed with Harry's plan, and they all took turns congratulating the lovely couple. An awful day had thankfully ended on a high note, and Flora couldn't be happier for her friends.

TWENTY-SEVEN

It was later that evening, when Will and Shona dropped Flora at her cold, dark cottage – Flora's own car was still sitting on Front Street where she had left it, and would have to wait till the morning. The thrill of Harry's proposal and all of the excited wedding planning that had followed, had now worn off, and Flora felt completely depleted of energy. She waved to the couple as the car drove off, letting herself into the coach house and turning on every light she passed to give her home a semblance of warmth. As was her new routine, Flora checked the mat for any more unwanted messages, and breathed a sigh of relief to see that there were none. Flicking the switch in the kitchen to turn on the central heating, she rushed straight into the small sitting room to see Reggie. He was in his cage where she had left him – locked in for once to allow him to properly recuperate – but he was sitting up straight and his tiny orange and black eyes were alert and tracked Flora as she entered the room. A small wiggle of his tail feather and a fluffing of his body preceded a long bout of clucking as Flora reached into the cage and Reggie jumped eagerly onto her hand.

"My Flora!" he squawked happily.

Flora peered at her feathered friend closely, keen to make sure he wasn't favouring either side, but he looked to be fine and normal.

"Aw Reggie, you're such a brave bird. Brave bird, brave bird," Flora repeated as she reached her free hand down to take off her shoes and relieve her tired feet.

"Brave bird!" Reggie repeated immediately, copying Flora's intonation perfectly.

Their sweet moment was interrupted by the doorbell, and Flora couldn't help but release a few words of dismay. She really didn't have either the energy or the inclination to deal with anyone else today, so Flora sat quietly and tapped Reggie's beak gently to give him the message he should stay silent for a moment too. Her shoulder throbbed where she had been kicked, and Flora couldn't face being sociable. She really wanted to take some of the painkillers the hospital had given her and sink into a warm bath. The bell rang again and then Flora's phone buzzed with a message. Reluctantly, Flora looked at it, jumping up with a sudden spurt of energy when she saw it was from Adam, saying he was outside her front door and would love to see her if she was home!

"Adam! I didn't think I'd see you today!" Flora exclaimed as she practically threw the door open to welcome him in.

"Aye, me neither, but Blackett said he had it all in hand, and the confession was quick enough to come by – that young lady wasn't quiet in railing about all the injustices she's suffered, believe me! She still doesn't really understand what she's done or what it will mean for her, she thinks she was justified in killing Ray," Adam raised both his eyebrows and his shoulders in a gesture that implied he really couldn't understand some people.

"She's so young," Flora said quietly, "I think she just wanted to be part of Ray's life, of village life, but it seems he told her in no uncertain terms that he had no space for her in his affections. It's all such a shame."

"Aye, that it is," Adam placed a large grocery bag on the kitchen counter and pulled Flora in for a big hug, "I couldn't wait until tomorrow, I hope you don't mind? I know you must be shattered. How's your shoulder? Did you get it checked over?"

"Yes, they said it was just badly bruised, thankfully it wasn't any closer to my collar bone or they said that could have been fractured by such a strong impact. Anyway, nothing to worry about. And of course I don't mind you dropping by, I'm never too tired to see you," Flora kissed him lightly on the lips and they made their way into the sitting room where Reggie was waiting. Even he didn't seem to have had enough energy to come to the front door.

"Here's the little man of the moment," Adam said, stroking Reggie's feathers lightly, "he's always looking out for you, isn't he? I didn't realise how handy a parrot could be!"

"Me neither! He certainly is a treasure, I wouldn't be without him now," Flora replied, managing a small smile, "Shall I make us something to eat? Or a cup of tea?"

"No, you just sit there. That bag I brought in is full of ready-made dishes of Chinese food from the Marks and Spencer food shop in Morpeth. I'll get it all heated up. There's a bottle of red in there too!"

Flora couldn't believe his thoughtfulness, when she knew Adam too must be exhausted, and she relaxed in her chair and let herself be cooked for and looked after for once.

The food eaten, the pair sat together on the couch. Flora's legs rested across Adam's lap and he rubbed her feet gently.

"Hopefully, now we can move on and get back to some sort of normality," Flora said, a sigh of relaxation escaping her lips.

"I should think so, we can leave all talk of investigations and focus on the future," Adam agreed, "one last word on that though – as I suspected, they didn't find any fingerprints on the note you were sent. Neither on the envelope nor on the sheet of paper itself. I'll ask Pat Hughes to have a word with Joe Stanton, but with no evidence, it can only really be an informal chat. It's very frustrating, sorry love, if you get anything else like that you must let me know immediately," Adam's mouth turned down with annoyance, presumably at the fact that he had been unable to prove anything and therefore the issue would have to be left unresolved for now.

"Anyway, how's the tearoom going?" Adam's face relaxed as he deliberately changed the subject and looked directly into Flora's eyes.

"Well, it's mostly still customers from the village, and only a few a day. Not enough to sustain me long term, though I do have longer term plans for the big house. I had a great idea the other day, though, it's linked to the children's stories I'm writing! I'm not sure if I've mentioned those, things have been a bit mad around here, and for you too!"

"They certainly have! Sounds intriguing though, tell me more," Adam rubbed her leg affectionately.

"Yes, I think I'm going to have the next stable block converted, the one that is attached to the back of the tearoom, and a door put in so that people can walk through from one to the other."

"To extend the tearoom?"

"No, to add a small bookshop and little library corner! I was thinking we could have book readings from authors, and I could promote my books of course, if I ever get as far as having them published! I'd need to find an illustrator first, and have them edited and... well, there's a lot of steps between now and then, but I'm excited by the project. We could have children's story time and..," Flora paused when she saw Adam smiling widely at her.

"I'm so happy for you, love, that sounds fantastic," he said, "it's lovely seeing your eyes sparkle again."

Flora blushed and ran her hands through her messy hair, pinning it behind her ears, "Thank you, it's good to have things to focus on and look forward to. Oh, that reminds me, you'll never guess what happened at the hospital!"

Flora went on to tell Adam all about Harry's proposal, and how it had seemed to breathe the life back into Betty's cheeks. The wedding planning was already underway, with the idea to have the ceremony in the hospital chapel as soon as Betty had recovered for a few days after her operation, with just a few close friends in attendance. Flora was already planning her outfit in her head! The older couple's joy had rubbed off on everyone there, and Flora had been happy to see Will and Shona looking more like their old selves, the relief evident on their faces all afternoon. She dearly hoped that Shona would be able to grieve her dad's death properly now, without the threat of arrest hanging over her, and that she could make a good go of it in the pub. Little Aaron deserved some stability, and to get back to his own bedroom.

"What's going on in that busy head of yours?" Adam asked gently, running his finger down Flora's cheek.

"Oh, just thinking about Shona and Aaron. She hasn't been able to grieve, or to be in her own home above the pub where she'll be surrounded by Ray everywhere she looks. It's good that she'll be able to get back there now and begin the process of healing and moving on."

"It is, and I'm sure that with the support of all her friends in the village, she'll be okay. She has Will, too, they seem like a good match."

"They do indeed," Flora agreed, snuggling in closer to Adam, feeling completely relaxed for the first time since the murder.

TWENTY-EIGHT

Flora dragged herself out of bed the next morning, her body protesting at even the slightest movement. She went through her morning routine on autopilot, wincing when the water from the shower hit her sore shoulder, that now sported a rather fetching deep blue and green hue. After phoning the hospital to see how Betty's night had been, and happy to hear she had been comfortable and managed some sleep, Flora made her way to the tearoom with Reggie on her shoulder. Thankfully, he himself seemed completely back to normal and chirped away happily, his little head bobbing up and down as he waddled along, from Flora's shoulder to the crook of her neck and back again. There was a heavy drizzle this day, so Flora had worn a light raincoat over her sweater dress and leggings, even opting for a pair of tan leather boots for

204

the first time this season.

The baked goods were waiting in their plastic box, as expected, and the familiarity of the task of setting out the cakes and crockery gave Flora a sense that today might hopefully be free from surprises. It was just past nine o'clock, when Harry appeared, unusually having come by car rather than walking from the village.

"Morning, Flora, just wanted to call in and say thank you again for yesterday. Goodness knows what would have happened if you hadn't arrived when you did!"

"I just wish I'd gotten there sooner, to be honest," Flora said as she pulled out a chair for Harry and moved to sit on the other side of the table.

"Sorry, I can't stay, on the way to the hospital to see my fiancée," Harry's cheeks flushed red as he said it, and Flora could tell how happy he was. It gave her a warm glow to think of him and Betty.

"Give Betty my love, and tell her I'll be in this evening to see her," Flora replied, "I called this morning and they said she's as comfortable as can be expected."

"Yes, I phoned too, I was worried because she's not good with using her mobile phone and wasn't answering my texts. Anyway, all well. Now, not wanting to relive anything or put a damper on things," Harry began carefully, and Flora almost physically winced, so little did she wish to talk about anything relating to the murder, "It's just that I had been planning to mention to you, even before everything happened yesterday, that the young lady in question hadn't transferred the money for the deposits on either the shop or the flat."

"So, do you think she didn't ever intend to proceed at all? Why would she sign the contract and how did she start fitting the shop out then?" Flora was full of questions, "I wonder if that's why she befriended Joe Stanton? – I can only think that they met at the fete – maybe he has been buying the supplies, the wood and everything, if she had promised to transfer the money straight back to him?"

"Quite possible. As for whether she intended to open the shop, I think she must have, yes. In her own mind, anyway – she was clearly delusional, embarking on a project like that with no money to invest up front," Harry obviously had his solicitor hat on now, Flora thought, "she clearly had an idea of how she wanted her life in the village to be, and just ploughed on regardless of any obstacles to that vision – poor Ray included."

"Well, with what has happened, and given she won't be progressing with it anyway, we'll just write off that money," Flora was quick to draw a line under the whole terrible saga, shuddering as a chill ran through her, "you could perhaps see if Joe wants any of the fixtures and fittings, otherwise we'll leave them for the next person."

"Good thinking, anyway, best be off, I'll be in touch later as soon as I have the time of Betty's operation, though they said yesterday evening that they think it's likely to take place tomorrow."

"Great, thanks Harry, the sooner Betty's on the other side of the surgery, and recuperating, the better."

"Absolutely!" Harry waved as he got in his car and Flora stood at the tearoom door until he'd driven away, spotting a small figure walking up the driveway towards her.

"Pepper, how are you?" Flora welcomed the other woman with a warm hug.

"I'm much better now that I don't have the black cloud of being a murder suspect hanging over me!" Pepper said, as the two women took a seat at the table nearest Reggie's perch. The bird himself jumped down to say hello to the new visitor, nuzzling her hand expectantly until Pepper began stroking his feathers.

"Welcome to the tearoom!" he squawked and both women laughed. This was a completely different version of Pepper to the one Flora had seen before now. She had some colour in her cheeks and her eyes seemed brighter and more focused on what was happening in the room.

"I just came to say thank you," Pepper began, when they both had a cup of tea and were sharing a fruit scone, "I heard about what happened yesterday. Such an awful end to the whole thing. You must still be in shock, I would think."

"Well, yes, as you can imagine, it was all so totally unexpected, and I'm so upset about what happened to Betty, I really wish things had turned out differently – in that respect at least."

"I can completely understand, I think it will probably take us all some time to get over what happened," Pepper rubbed Flora's arm gently in a gesture of solidarity.

"It certainly will. But, moving on to happier things, you mentioned the other day that you were planning to see your daughter over Christmas? It must be lovely to be reconciled again."

"Yes, actually we're going up next weekend, just for a few days, to see our Anna and her husband, as well as our beautiful new granddaughter. Anna's sent me pictures of course, by email, and I know I'm biased, but little Ruby is absolutely gorgeous!"

"That's so lovely, I'm so happy for you and George."

"Thank you, that's the other part of why I popped up here, actually," Pepper said, beginning to look slightly uncomfortable and fidgeting with her napkin.

"Oh?"

"Yes, as we'll definitely be up in Scotland over Christmas, and since you did so well organising the fete at such short notice…"

Flora wasn't sure she liked the sound of where this was headed.

"Well," Pepper continued after a pause, "I was wondering if you would take over my role as organiser of the village Talent Show, 'Baker's Rise Stars in their Eyes'? I can give you my checklist of everything that's involved in the production."

Given that the woman seemed to have turned a corner with her own wellbeing, and that Flora didn't have a good enough reason to say no, she felt she had no choice but to agree.

"Perfect, thank you so much, Flora, I'm sure you'll have fun, and you'll get to meet more of the locals!"

Flora wasn't so sure it would be that enjoyable an experience – it certainly seemed like a lot of extra work – but she simply nodded and smiled, whilst sipping her tea and wondering if there was ever a 'normal' day to be had in Baker's Rise!

By lunchtime, Flora had been visited by Billy Northcote, Tanya, Will and Shona, all popping by separately to thank her, to check on her, or both. It was lovely to have friends who cared, but Flora had found the morning quite tiring, particularly in light of how exhausted she already was after the previous day's events. Deciding to treat herself to an afternoon's rest and relaxation, she closed the tearoom early, dropped Reggie at the coach house and then walked down the hill to Front Street, intending to collect her car after calling into Baker's Rise Cuts and Dyes for the long-awaited and much anticipated haircut! She wanted to look her best for Betty and Harry's upcoming ceremony.

Amy was sitting in the quiet salon reading a book as Flora entered, the bell over the door tinkling loudly.

"Flora, what a lovely surprise, I hear you're our village hero!"

"Well, no not a hero, but I'm certainly glad the village can quieten down a bit now!" Flora smiled, sitting in the large chair which Amy indicated.

"So, what can I do for you today?" the younger woman asked, "just a trim or something more?"

"Actually," Flora said, feeling suddenly brave, "I think I'd like to go back to my original chin-length bob, but with some colour too, maybe a couple of different browns running through it to hide the grey and a blonder highlight?"

"Ooh, that sounds gorgeous," Amy's enthusiasm was contagious, and Flora immediately felt happy with her rash decision, "You'll look fabulous!" she gushed as began preparing everything. Flora sat back in the chair and closed her eyes, trying to let the strain of the past weeks drain from her tired muscles.

TWENTY-NINE

Happier with her new look than she'd thought she could be, Flora left the hairdressers feeling lighter in both body and spirit. She'd had a lovely chat with Amy, and learnt more about her partner Gareth, and his little son Lewis. Flora had only met Gareth once before, at the afternoon tea event to celebrate the opening of the tearoom. Amy explained how he lived a couple of miles outside the village and she still lived with her parents in the centre of Baker's Rise, though the couple were saving to get a house together. Amy's happy chatter, combined with the lovely cup of tea she had made, distracted Flora from her own thoughts, making the whole experience thoroughly enjoyable. Now, Flora needed to grab a few groceries from Baker's Rise Essential Supplies, rescue her car from where she had dumped it yesterday before the big showdown with Emma, and then go home to continue her stress-free afternoon.

A grand plan. Or rather, it would have been, had Flora not quite literally bumped into Joe Stanton as he was leaving the very shop she wanted to go into. Flora cast her eyes to the ground, her shoulders hunched, really not wanting any confrontation with the man. Apparently, that was not to be, as he stood where he was on seeing her, his frame blocking the small doorway and giving Flora no choice but to look up at him to see if he was going to move.

"So, who do we have here? The great Lady of the Manor herself," Joe said scornfully, leaning against the door frame as if he had all the time in the world to harass Flora.

"Let me past," Flora ground out.

"Not so quick, Mrs. la-de-da Miller. I think you owe me an apology, don't you?"

"An apology?" Flora asked incredulously, squaring her shoulders and looking him straight in the eye. A bubble of anger rose up from her stomach and she felt her fists curl up into balls, "Why on earth would I be apologising to you? Surely it should be the other way around?"

Ignoring her last question, Joe spat back," First, you lose me my job…"

"Ah, hold on," Flora interjected, her voice rising with indignation, "You lost that yourself from partaking in illegal postal activity!"

"Then," Joe continued as if he hadn't heard Flora, "my wife leaves me…"

"Again, nothing to do with me," Flora stood her ground, "I can only sympathise with the woman if this is the way you behave!"

"Thirdly," Joe was shouting now, his temper close to fraying, "you lose me both my new girlfriend and the job at her shop!"

"New girlfriend? You could only have met her a couple of weeks ago, she'd never been to the village before that! And don't think for a minute that she really liked you – you were just a handy man in more ways than one!" Flora took a step back, worried by the look in the man's eyes.

"Why you…!" Joe advanced two large steps towards the retreating Flora.

"That's enough, Joe," the steadying tones of Pat Hughes came from behind Flora for the second time in as many days. She really would have to get the man a gift or something to thank him, Flora decided, as she tried to calm her erratic breathing, "Is he bothering you, Flora?"

"He is certainly being rather accusatory – groundless I might add – and, as you can see, aggressive," Flora said, only half turning to face the local policeman, as she didn't wish to turn her back completely on Joe, not trusting him for a minute.

"Well, it's a good thing that I was just looking for Mr. Stanton here," Pat said, staring pointedly at the other man, "we need to have a little chat, you and I."

Flora stood aside as Pat indicated Joe should follow him back down the street, all the while Joe himself was casting daggers in her direction. She stood her ground, not flinching as he walked past her, far too close for her liking, and only then did Flora feel her nerves shred completely and the trembling in her body begin.

"Are you okay, dear?" the voice from behind Flora made her jump, and she turned to see Jean Sykes who ran the shop, no doubt wanting to see where the cold draught was coming from.

"Yes, thank you, sorry the door's been open for so long," Flora tried to gather her wits.

"Not at all, what can I get you? I hear you've had an eventful week already, and it's only Tuesday!" the kindly woman, with her short white hair, smiling eyes and beautiful Scottish lilt, always made Flora feel at ease whenever she shopped there.

"That's an understatement!" Flora managed a smile and they were soon chatting like old friends, reminding Flora that most of the people in the small Baker's Rise community were friendly and welcoming.

"You must come up to the tearoom soon," Flora invited, as she was leaving, before rushing to her nearby car to escape to the anonymity of home and her feathered friend.

THIRTY

The following Monday, Flora dressed in a beautiful purple satin dress and matching bolero jacket – purchased a few years previously for a cruise trip she and Gregory were taking – with a hat she had found in Morpeth at the weekend. It was almost exactly the same shade of purple, and Flora had squealed when she saw it as she and Adam browsed the shops. Adam had very quickly come to realise that Flora had a certain weakness for clothes and accessories! In a very sweet gesture he had even bought her a beautiful silver pendant with a large amethyst stone set in the centre – the perfect final addition to her outfit.

Now, they both stood in the small hospital chapel, with Will and Shona, Pat and Tanya, Lily and Stan, Billy Northcote and the widowed shopkeeper Jean Sykes, who had known Betty for years both in the village and the local branch of the Women's Institute. Reverend Marshall stood at the front of the tiny aisle with Harry, the groom looking resplendent in a grey three-piece suit, complete with purple cravat and matching handkerchief in his top pocket. The only indication of Harry's nerves were his repeated checking in his pocket, for the small ring box which he had stored there. There was no best man, and no bridesmaids, at the couple's request, as they wanted a small ceremony with no fuss. Sally Marshall had very kindly offered to take some photographs, and Flora had food waiting in the family room attached to Betty's hospital ward for them all to share afterwards. Betty herself would be in hospital a few more days, until they were sure she could manage at home with Harry's help.

A recording of the wedding march, provided by the vicar, began playing from the small music system in the corner of the room as Betty appeared. She was being pushed by the ward Sister in a wheelchair which Flora and Tanya had decorated in delicate purple ribbons and fresh blooms. Betty herself was wearing a long, loose-fitting dress which she had asked Flora to find her on her shopping trip. Luckily, it had fit perfectly and, more importantly, Betty had been able to get into it comfortably with her new hip. The cream dress, dotted with small, embroidered sprigs of lavender, set off Betty's grey hair and light eyes beautifully. Ordinarily, Flora liked nothing more than a mission to find the perfect occasion ware, but in this case the tight deadline and desire that it should meet Betty's exacting requirements, had left Flora fretting until she had found the dress and a beautiful purple wrap to match.

Bride and groom smiled widely, and more than a few tears were shed amongst the small congregation as the couple said their vows. Adam squeezed Flora's hand and smiled down at her, as she looked at him through watery eyes. It was all so lovely, and so romantic, that Flora couldn't hide her own emotions.

"Well, at least something good came out of that horrible situation," Billy spoke up when they were all sitting with cups of tea and slices of a wedding cake kindly provided by Lily.

"It certainly did," Harry agreed, smiling dotingly on his new wife, "and as soon as Betty here is fit and well again, we'll be taking the cruise she's always dreamed of to celebrate!"

"Really?" Clearly this was the first time Betty had heard the news, and she was both surprised and delighted.

"Absolutely, you choose where to and I'll book it," Harry said indulgently.

"Congratulations!" Flora said again, for about the fifth time since the service, kissing Betty and then Harry gently on the cheek. She couldn't be more thrilled for the couple, and hoped with all her heart that this signalled the start of happier times in Baker's Rise.

Join Flora and Reggie in "Absence Makes the Heart Grow Fondant", the next instalment in the Baker's Rise Mysteries series, to see whether happier times are indeed on their way!

Absence Makes the Heart Grow Fondant

Baker's Rise Mysteries Book Three

Publication Date 21st December 2021

The third instalment of the cosy Baker's Rise series is here, with Flora and Reggie facing some ghosts from the past!

Fresh from her latest investigation, Lady of the Manor Flora is looking forward to a quiet Autumn, writing her children's stories, serving customers in the tearoom, and learning how to make and decorate a traditional Christmas cake in time for the festive season.

What she doesn't anticipate is the arrival of her ex-husband, declaring his undying love for her! Is he as lovesick as he declares, or does he have another reason for seeking Flora out?

Of course, in true Baker's Rise style, things get rather more complicated rather quickly, and Flora finds herself in the eye of a whole new storm.

Packed with humour and suspense, colourful characters and a sprinkle of romance, this next Baker's Rise Mystery will certainly leave you hungry for more!

(Includes a Christmas Cake recipe!)

R. A. Hutchins

ABOUT THE AUTHOR

Rachel Hutchins lives in northeast England with her husband, three children and their dog Boudicca. She loves writing both mysteries and romances, and enjoys reading these genres too! Her favourite place is walking along the local coastline, with a coffee and some cake!

You can connect with Rachel and sign up to her monthly newsletter via her website at: www.authorrachelhutchins.com

Alternatively, she has social media pages on:

Facebook: www.facebook.com/rahutchinsauthor

Instagram: www.instagram.com/ra_hutchins_author

Twitter: www.twitter.com/hutchinsauthor

R. A. Hutchins

OTHER BOOKS BY R. A. HUTCHINS

"Counting down to Christmas"

Rachel has published a collection of twelve contemporary romance stories, all set around Christmas, and with the common theme of a holiday happily-ever-after. Filled with humour and emotion, they are sure to bring a sparkle to your day!

"To Catch A Feather" (Found in Fife Book One)

When tragedy strikes an already vulnerable Kate Winters, she retreats into herself, broken and beaten. Existing rather than living, she makes a journey North to try to find herself, or maybe just looking for some sort of closure.

Cameron McAllister has known his own share of grief and love lost. His son, Josh, is now his only priority. In his forties and running a small coffee shop in a tiny Scottish fishing village, Cal knows he is unlikely to find love again.

When the two meet and sparks fly, can they overcome their past losses and move on towards a shared future, or are the memories which haunt them still too real?

These books, as well as others by Rachel, can be found on Amazon worldwide in e-book and paperback formats, as well as free to read on Kindle Unlimited.

R. A. Hutchins

Made in the USA
Monee, IL
23 July 2023

39766103R00128